COUNTRY DANCE

PARTHIAN
LIBRARY OF WALES

Margiad Evans (Peggy Whistler) was born in Uxbridge in 1909, and lived in the Border area in Ross-on-Wye. The border was central to her consciousness, and she adopted the Welsh nom de plume, Margiad Evans, out of a sense of identity with Wales. She attended Hereford School of Art, but although she continued to paint and draw until late in her life, writing displaced art as her primary work. In addition to *Country Dance* (1932), her novels include *The Wooden Doctor* (1933), *Turf or Stone* (1934) and *Creed* (1936). She also wrote numerous articles and short stories, some of which were collected in *The Old and The Young* (1948), and two collections of poetry, *Poems from Obscurity* (1947) and *A Candle Ahead* (1956). Her *Autobiography* was published in 1943 and *A Ray of Darkness*, an account of her experience of epilepsy, appeared in 1952. She died in 1958.

COUNTRY DANCE

MARGIAD EVANS

LIBRARY OF WALES

Parthian
The Old Surgery
Napier Street
Cardigan
SA43 1ED
www.parthianbooks.co.uk

The Library of Wales is a Welsh Assembly Government
initiative which highlights and celebrates Wales' literary
heritage in the English language.

Published with the financial support of
the Welsh Books Council.

The Library of Wales publishing project is based at
Trinity College, Carmarthen, SA31 3EP.
www.libraryofwales.org

Series Editor: Dai Smith

First published in 1932
© C. E. Davis 1932
Library of Wales edition published 2006
Foreword © Catrin Collier 2005
All Rights Reserved

ISBN 1-902638-84-0
    9 781902 638829

Cover design by Marc Jennings
Cover image and illustrations by Peggy Whistler

Printed and bound by Dinefwr Press, Llandybïe, Wales
Typeset by Lucy Llewellyn

British Library Cataloguing in Publication Data

A cataloguing record for this book is available from the British
Library.

FOREWORD

A fellow writer once showed me a set of ten beautifully bound diaries she had discovered in a second-hand bookshop in Hay-on-Wye. Written in elegant copper-plate script by a farmer's wife during the first thirty years of the twentieth century, they were decorated with pictures of royalty, flowers and Gibson girls cut from magazines. The pages were perfumed with the scent of long dead, pressed summer flowers, which added to the seductive promise of a glimpse into a vanished world.

The diaries emphasized the narrow confines of rural life in Wales during the first half of the twentieth century. Possibly the most dynamic entry was written on Saturday July 1st, 1916:

> Rose early, milked cows. Weather fine. Packed cart. Changed into second best dress. Took bacon, plucked chickens, butter and cheese to market. Bought new hat.

Nothing, not even the Great War, existed for that woman outside of her husband's farm and its immediate vicinity. She noted the passing of the seasons, the vagaries of weather, prices at local markets and the purchase of every garment. National and international events passed her by. For her they held no relevance.

The life recorded in those diaries, like those of the characters in the novella *Country Dance*, belongs to a society that has ceased to exist in memory, but traces linger – on the written page, in contemporary documents, and in the imaginations of historians and writers, such as that of Margiad Evans, who obviously knew it well and used that knowledge to produce *Country Dance*.

It was a world in which horizons were marked by the distance that could be travelled – and back – in a day, in which disaster was the hired boy pouring hot, not cold water into a churn and spoiling the butter, and in which chapel or church – depending on whether you were Welsh or English – was the highlight of the week. Excitement was a child falling into a river and almost drowning before being rescued, and marriage and courtship were the most important events in life outside of birth and death.

The novella opens with an introduction and brief biography of Ann Goodman, 'a country-woman to the backbone', born of an English father and Welsh mother. Brought up on a farm in the Welsh mountains, she returns to her birthplace in the Border country to live with her parents in 1850. We are given a description of the derelict shepherd's cottage where she was born:

> the garden where she worked is overrun with weeds...
> sheep crop around the doorstep... the chimneys have
> fallen... the fireplaces choked with fallen plaster... and
> only the stone benches remain as they were when she
> was alive.

It requires very little imagination to picture Peggy Whistler taking on the mantle of her alter-ego, Margiad Evans, walking the beautiful Border country and stumbling across the ruin that had been reduced to serving as a store for apples. Perhaps the writer sat on one of the benches, and gazed at the vista that would have been familiar to Ann. Perhaps she pictured the shepherd's daughter looking to the Welsh mountains and thinking of her lovers... the English shepherd and the Welsh farmer who was 'her father's master'.

'Ann's Book' follows the brief introduction and is penned, diary style, in the present tense. She begins to write in 1850, when she leaves her cousin's farm at Twelve Poplars in Wales, to care for her ailing Welsh mother in England. Her fiancé, the 'English' shepherd Gabriel, gives her the book as a parting gift '... to write in it all I do, for him to see, until we shall be married'.

In the book, Ann begins to chronicle the minutiae of farming life that changed little between the setting of *Country Dance* in 1850, and 1932, when Margiad Evans wrote the novella.

Ann meets a parson and her father's master, who is 'hard and sharp... two men I do hate'. She recalls her brother who 'died grown up and married', and attends a barn dance, where the master notices her. Her mother dies, her father rejects her, and when she travels to Wales for her mother's funeral she returns to Twelve Poplars, close to her fiancé and far from the master, yet her affection for Gabriel has not survived their separation.

An outing to sheepdog trials proves to be one of the highlights of Ann's book and life, but then the two protagonists are Ann's father and fiancé, and her father is representing the hot-headed master who has noticed Ann and dared to speak to her, to Gabriel's chagrin.

From the first page there is a sense of foreboding. Ann's life is a tragedy waiting to happen – the only question is what form it will take. From the outset we know that Ann's lover is a jealous and exacting man who demands she give him an account of everyone she meets and talks to during their separation, and there is little humour in *Country Dance* to relieve the sense of impending doom – a few episodes chronicling the mishaps of an inept farm boy, Charlie, but even through those we have a sense of approaching disaster.

This simple story of lovers' rivalry mirrors the conflict between Welsh and English in the land that borders the two countries. On the one hand we have the ancient language and farming ways of the Celts; on the other, the anglicised ways of the Saxon English. Yet the division is not so great when both factions live the rural life that was doomed to disappear with the advent of mechanisation.

In *Country Dance* Margiad Evans gives us a glimpse of old rural Wales and life in the Border country even more potent than the faint scent of flowers pressed almost a century ago. While we read, we see again the isolated shepherd tending his flock on the hillside, feel the anxiety and terror of bankruptcy that accompanies an outbreak of sheep scab, and sleep under a hedge with a farm labourer turned drunk because he cannot face the finality of his wife's death.

Margiad Evans wrote to considerable critical and popular success during her lifetime. The Riverrun Press edition of *Country Dance* on my desk is a 1978 reprint of the original 1932 edition published by Arthur Barker – a London publisher. On the back is a brief author biography that begins: 'The years since the death of Margiad Evans in 1958 have not been kind to the reputation of a poet and novelist who was widely acclaimed in the 40s and 50s...'

I grew up in Wales in the 1950s and 60s, yet her work was never mentioned at my school or in the local library. Whenever I asked the eternal question 'What should I read next?' I was directed towards Russian, English, American, German and French novelists. I discovered a few – a precious few – Welsh authors for myself, which only added weight to my teachers's pronouncement that 'people like you (translate as South Wales Valley born) don't write'.

Peggy Whistler/Margiad Evans was born in 1909 and died in 1958, but though she was widely read and admired, she fell out of favour and her books went out of print. I look forward to revisiting her world in the future, and also entering those of other fellow Welsh writers who are thankfully not forgotten, due to the Library of Wales series.

Catrin Collier

ILLUSTRATIONS

COUNTRY DANCE

Dod dy law ond wyd yn coelio
Dan fy mron a gwilia 'mrifo
Ti gei glywed os gwrandewi
Sŵn y galon fach yn torri.

Place thy hand, unless thou believest me,
Under my breast and beware of hurting me;
Thou shalt hear if thou listen
The sound of the little heart breaking.

OLD SONG

INTRODUCTION

The struggle for supremacy in her mixed blood is the unconscious theme of Ann Goodman's book.

She writes of Gabriel, her sweetheart, English, jealous and sullen; of Evan ap Evans, her father's master, Welsh, violent and successful; of Olwen Davies, whose strange, whimsical beauty became the talk of the Border.

She was a country-woman to the backbone, hence the absence of rustic description: floods, winds, storms, and sunshine were as natural and unremarkable to her as to a bird. Of the human mind and temper she was an acute observer.

Born of an English father and a Welsh mother, brought up on a farm in the mountains, she returned for a brief period to her border birthplace: at her sweetheart's request she wrote down her actions and sayings, as a concession to his jealous disposition. This only roused it to fury. Once formed, however, she continued the habit, and to that and my discovery of her book I owe my true knowledge of a tragedy which, tricked out and distorted by tradition, has been handed down among us: chance threw me the facts, and I grasped them with eagerness.

Circumstances have dimmed the memory of this woman and ironically accentuated that of the rivals, Gabriel Ford and Evan ap Evans, shepherd and farmer, Englishman and Welshman. The glare which at her death picked them out with horrible distinctness has left her curiously nebulous and unreal, a mere motive of tragedy. Even today, nearly seventy years later, anyone of our countryside will describe either of the men from hearsay. Only one very old man remembers her face because as a boy he loved it.

The shepherd's cottage where Ann was born is falling to ruin on top of the hill. I wish that it were not so far gone, that the garden where she worked were not overrun with weeds. The garden walls have vanished, sheep crop around the doorstep, and only the two stone benches remain as they were when she was alive. The chimneys have fallen, the wind and rain make free with the windows, inside it is not safe to tread the narrow staircase, and the fireplaces are choked with fallen plaster.

The present owner uses the place for storing apples: he has had most of the rubbish cleaned away, and a pleasant smell lingers there even in summer.

From Ann's benches, one either side of the gaping door, miles of country can be seen over the roofs of the farm: the winding road to Salus, broadened and macadamised, dipping and rising, the river and the bridge, Salus itself backed by two low hills, again the river meandering yet swift, in winter a red torrent spread sullenly abroad, then away, away to Wales, where turned the eyes of Myfanwy to the mountains whence she came.

It may seem remarkable that Ann in her writing makes use of only the present tense. It must be remembered that the entries were made over a space of months, and at the beginning were intended to take the place of speech between her and her sweetheart. Her part of the world, for one reason or another, has preserved little dialect and fewer turns of speech, but the custom of referring to past events as though they were at the moment occurring still survives, and doubtless would be even more prevalent in her day. To me this lends additional strength and vividness to her records, and at times even gives me the uncomfortable feeling of listening at a keyhole.

Curious people may express surprise that a shepherd's daughter, born nearly a hundred years ago, should attain such proficiency in reading and writing. For my part I can only add that I am glad that it was so.

Margiad Evans

ANN'S BOOK

FIRST PART
1850

ANN'S BOOK

FIRST PART
1850

Gabriel gives me this book, telling me to write in it all I do, for him to see, until we shall be married. And when that will be I do not know, since I am to leave Twelve Poplars and look to my mother.

Owen Somers comes for me: Mary and I cry. I have lived with her for fifteen years. The morning is bitter cold and the horse will not stand still for me to get in. Owen wraps my feet in straw, but they are frozen before we have gone very far. At first we talk, the last half of the way I sleep, and he wakes me at the foot of the hill: I stumble up half asleep. There is a light in the kitchen window and my father and mother are having their tea. Afterwards I wash up. My father says there are lambs about already; we are later in the hills. Even my mother is up at five, and when we have given my father his breakfast, he lights his lantern and goes off to his sheep. Evan ap Evans says that he is very content with them this year: my father says a wiser man would have waited before he spoke, with the lambing ahead, but the master can never hold his tongue or his temper.

I miss my dairy. With everything out of the way so soon there is a lot of time to spare. While I am sewing the new curtains for the kitchen I see the parson come up the hill in the snow. My mother goes to let him in, and he sits himself down before the fire to thaw a bit and drink the cup of tea we give him. My lap is full of snips and ends, which I drop all over the floor when I stand up.

'And this is your daughter? We have met before, I think?'

'Maybe,' says my mother.

'And how does she like these parts after the hills?'

'She likes them well enough.'

'And how long are you thinking of staying?' he asks me.

'Until she shall be married.'

He laughs a little. I can see he thinks I have lost my tongue, leaving my mother to answer all the questions. She smiles at me.

'And whom are you marrying? Is it anyone here?'

'It's Gabriel Ford,' says my mother.

'I don't know him. Is he English?'

'What else could he be with such a name?' cries my mother. 'He is not from these parts, but where she has come from.'

'The mountains, eh? It's a long way for a sweetheart.'

'Shorter than for others, perhaps.'

'Perhaps you are right, Mrs. Goodman. But the men hereabouts are well enough. Don't you think so?'

'Maybe, but my husband and Evan ap Evans are the only ones worth a look.'

Parson gives her a sharp glance: 'Ah, Evan ap Evans is a fine-looking man, I grant you, but he belongs to the chapel.'

'He's a true Welshman,' says my mother. 'What else should he belong to?'

'Well, well,' mutters Parson, pushing back his chair. 'You will be better when the warmer weather comes, Mrs. Goodman.'

'I hope so, I'm sure, but I'd rather be higher up.'

'Why, what do you mean? You are on top of the hill as it is. It's quite a climb.'

'Brenin Mawr! It's nothing but a pimple,' cries my mother.

Parson laughs. 'Have you met any neighbours yet, Ann?'

'Yes, sir. I met most of them before I went away, and I have seen them on visits.'

'Ah, they do not change much. This is a quiet spot.'

'My son was alive then,' says my mother.

I often think of Rhys, who died grown up and married when I was no more than fifteen; my mother loved him heart and soul, for it seemed he was all her child. One hard winter like this he was out of nights with the early lambing and he took a chill and died, leaving Gwyneth to follow him two months later when their first child was born. They say seeing him with his sheep was like watching a man with his family; that comes from my father, who has shepherding in his blood.

11

Another person comes today. This is the sexton's daughter, all arms and legs, as thin as a hurdle. She comes to see if our hens are laying; her father will have eggs, and whence to find them this weather she does not know without going to Salus, and he will not let her half a mile from home. All the parish knows what a life he leads her.

The cold is in my very bones. I make such a great fire in the kitchen that the chimney catches: the smoke rushes out and goes away on the wind till everybody thinks we are burning. Half the parish comes running with pails of snow and sticks to beat it out: even the master is there to see his cottage burn. My mother runs out in her stockings; her feet are so swollen she cannot wear boots. Never was there such a scrimmage over a chimney!

I throw salt on the fire, and when my father comes it is out; he is very angry, and so is the master. He takes me by the shoulders before all the world. He has a Welsh voice that sings in speaking in English.

'Next time, look, my girl, what you are about.'

I step back and say my sorrow, for I think of my father, but I hate Evan ap Evans from this day and wish Gabriel had been there to shake the life out of him.

Another heavy fall of snow and three of the lambs are dead. I am taking some sewing because the master is charging us with the cost of the chimney. And it is but scorched!

I find there is no yeast for Thursday's baking, so I leave my mother sitting before the fire with her knitting and the door locked, because my father will be late, and go to Salus to fetch some.

It is very dark and windy in the narrow lanes; when I cross the bridge I can hear the water is very near the top of the arches, and a glimmering here and there down in the meadows shows me the floods are out. Salus is empty, and well it may be on such a wild night; I get my yeast and am glad to set my feet on the way home, but the wind is dead against me and every inch is a struggle: the rain is falling in torrents so that it almost blinds me. I hear Tom Hill's cart coming; I know it by its one light and the clicking of the mare's hoofs. The light flickers over me, and Tom pulls up, calling me by name.

'What is wrong?' I shout above the din of the wind and rain.

'Sexton's missing – been off all day. We think he's in the river. Stop Olwen if you should meet her on your way back and take her home along with you.'

'That child out alone tonight!'

'Ay. She wanted to come with me. I told her there was nothing she could do, but I believe she followed me.'

'In the river!' I think of the awful sucking under the bridge, and the watery fields.

'I'll take her home. What are you going to do?' I ask.

'Going to Salus to find if anyone has seen him.'

He drives off. Half-way home I find Olwen sitting on a gate, soaked to the bone, without shawl or bonnet: she gives a great start when she sees me.

'Come home with me,' I says.

'Ann, I can't go farther, I'm too affeared. Have they found him in the river?'

'No, Olwen. Come home, and you shall sleep the night with me. You have no cause to be affeared with me.'

'Ann, why did he do it? Last week, when he dug old Mr. Somers's grave, he laughed and said he would see all the parish underground.'

'It may not be so bad, after all. Come with me. Come home out of the cold.'

'Yes,' she answers, 'I'll go with you tonight, if Shepherd won't be vexed. I can't stay alone.'

My father is out till early morning looking for Sexton with the rest of the men. I see lights going up and down, and the master's dog is howling loud, as he always does when he is left behind. I cannot sleep, though Olwen, tired out, goes off beside me the minute the candle is blown out, and when my father comes in I get up and make a cup of tea.

'There is seventeen foot of flood-water at the bridge,' he says, 'and the oak meadow is under. It's the highest for years. There's not a mite to be gained by searching. He'll turn up right in the morning.'

But three days later they find him, when the floods have gone down, fast in the hedge where the waters have carried him. The coroner sits over him; he says he was mad when he did it, for it seems he was mortal ill and all the world hard on him for his bad temper.

Olwen is still with us, and my father begins to grumble about the girl being no kin of ours. Mrs. Hill says she will have her at Baysham to mind the baby.

This morning, as I am walking at the bottom of the hill,

there I catch the master shouting at the gypsies that are on his land. He is waving his stick, they are looking rough, and I hear him cry out:

'Get off my land, or I'll make you!'

The gypsies give a murmur among themselves.

'Those that won't work shan't live,' shouts the master.

One of the women gives a sudden sharp screech: a knife flashes past him and falls at my feet. I pick it up. 'Give that to me,' orders Evan ap Evans very sharply. 'I'll have the law on them for that. They shall sweat for it next assizes.'

I give it to him; he puts it in his pocket.

'You are witness of attempted murder.'

'I am no such thing,' I says, not wishing to fall foul of the gypsies or get tangled up with the law. 'I didn't see the knife flung. I was stood here and it falls at my feet.'

'Then nobody flung it; it fell down from the clouds, I suppose?'

'*You* may have done, for aught I know,' I bursts out, fairly furious, master or no master, 'and it may have been meant for me.'

His mouth falls open; I pass him and go on up the hill, leaving him hammer and tongs with the gypsies. They seem to be getting the best of it, and well I wish they may.

How long is spring in coming!

The month has come in like a lion: four chimneys are blown down – one at Cotterill's, two at Baysham, where Olwen goes with many tears, and Mrs. Somers's copper chimney, which she says makes washing-day a nightmare.

I am close by Cotterill's when their chimney comes down with a noise like thunder; the bricks are scattered all over the yard, and the master runs out of the wagon-house. We stare at the broken chimney-stack.

'You bring ill-luck to chimneys,' says the master. 'Are you a witch, Ann Goodman?'

'I shall not have to pay for this one,' I answer.

He scowls.

All the Somers family are busy sawing up the great elm that has fallen across their pigsties. Owen is going to help on his uncle's farm come midsummer; they say he is wiser than his father, who is a fool with animals and fears his wife.

Gabriel tells me I sing well, but this morning my father hears me and calls out: 'Not so much concert, and get on with what you are doing.'

It is a little hard that he should never open his mouth but to grumble and find fault with all I do. My mother is poorly too, and keeps to her bed. I hang the new curtains in her window today, white ones with red roses. When I pull them for her to sleep, she says: 'They are pretty, Ann, but I would rather see the mountains. Indeed, they look a long way off today.' And I draws them back again.

Chimneys are a plague! We are sitting by the fire, and a great lump of soot falls down among the cinders, scattering them in my father's cider that is warming. He says it is loosened by the great wind, but the chimney must be dirty, and I am to sweep it.

I am up early, cutting young hazel rods in which the juice is rising; I tuft them well at their heads with bits of bushy

16

holly; when I have finished, I have brushes supple as leather, but upright. With these I sweep the chimney clean, and the fire burns clear and hot. The dirt and soot on me forces me to take a bath in the wash-tub. My mother is afraid of chills; it is a backward spring and early for baths.

Evan ap Evans loses all his prize fowls last week, stolen by the gypsies out of spite. What a black rage he is in! Not a word to a soul for three days after would he speak. My father says speak softly to gypsies, but the master cannot do that; it is not in his breed.

Parson comes, and I am busy in the garden with my skirts tucked up almost to my knees out of the dirt. He laughs; I am too ashamed to stand upright, for I must look a sight, with my long legs and my hair down on my shoulders. This man does seem to creep about.

'You are busy. How pretty your garden looks!'

I am pleased to hear that, for I have taken a deal of trouble with it.

'I have heard Mrs. Goodman isn't well. Is she in bed?'

'Yes, and has been this fortnight.'

He looks at me sharply. I go on scratching among the plants with my head down and my hair all over my face.

'I am sorry for that. I would have come before if I had known.'

'You should have known.'

He bends down and says: 'You are a queer woman. I don't think you are very civil, Ann; one can see you have lived in the mountains. Shall I go in and talk to your mother?'

My mother stares at my clothes; I am more than decent, but I burn with shame as Parson fixes his eyes on

17

me. I go downstairs, let down my dress, and put up my hair; in my vexation I break the new brown teapot, banging about getting my father's tea. When Parson comes down, I offer him a cup.

'Why, where's the gypsy?' he asks.

'What gypsy?'

'The one I met in the garden.'

'I am not a child, sir.'

He stops his laughing.

'No, indeed, you are not. I did not mean to annoy you, and you need not look so angry.'

I do not feel polite; as he goes out he has to unlatch the door himself; he turns back in the porch, saying over his shoulder:

'But you make a very pretty gypsy with your curls down.'

My father calls him a fool. He and Evan ap Evans are two men I do hate.

The evenings do draw out. Mrs. Hill gives me some seeds, and I spend hours in the garden planting them and pulling up the weeds. Sometimes the master passes. He speaks to me always in Welsh, and often I make believe not to hear him. Then he comes, leans his elbows on the wall, and says in his tongue:

'Good day, my proud girl.'

Laughing, he goes away. Why does he always speak to me in Welsh? I wish Gabriel would come! Tonight all the parish is dancing in the Somers's big barn. I see the Morgans from Gillow, the Meredyths, and the Willets. The Lewises are there beside the folk, and Miss Evans

18

has come with her brother. He has on a very fine waistcoat, with silk flowers, which he does not wear to chapel, although he goes very regular: perhaps his sister thinks it is not quiet enough for that, as they are so narrow in their ways. But the master pays no heeds to man or woman.

They have piled the hay into one corner: lamps and flares hang from the beams. Will Williams and Harry Parry are playing the concertina, and a young woman they say comes from the forest has a violin. More for show than playing, for when the master asks her to dance, she just puts her hand in his and whirls away with the rest, leaving the poor violin to Tom Somers, who soon breaks a string and puts all our teeth on edge.

It is pretty to see them all go round in the light, but I do not dance. Mrs. Hill tells me she does not feel comfortable so close to a man so be he is not her husband. We are both surprised to hear the master laughing behind us, where he has been stood listening to every word we have said, like the Welshman he is. 'Why, that's just it,' he says; 'if Ann will come along with me I'll soon teach her to dance.'

'Will you go, my dear?' asks Mrs. Hill. 'You will be cold stood still in that thin dress. Look at the lamps flickering.'

'No,' I says, 'I'll stay here.'

Evan ap Evans catches at my arm:

'Wilt thou dance with me, sweetheart?'

I answer him boldly in Welsh:

'No, for my heart goes with my feet,' and I think of Gabriel.

'Then you shall dance with me, fy nghariad anwyl, until

19

the day breaks.'

'That I will not.'

I sets my back against the wall.

'Very well, I am sorry,' says he, turning away.

'Why do you speak Welsh to me?'

'Because I am a Welshman.'

'But I am English.'

'Half. No, not that even, for you have lived in the mountains.'

He sings softly, in the voice that the English have not, an old Welsh song that I have sung round the fire at night.

Mrs. Hill smiles, for she cannot understand the tongue, but I feel the tears come smarting. I turn my head away.

'Ann, wilt thou dance?' repeats the master.

'You had better dance, Ann,' Mrs. Hill whispers. 'You can tread well on his toes.'

'More likely he will tread on mine. No, sir, you must find someone else; I am not going to dance.'

He goes away; I think I am to be left in peace, as the young lady from the forest clings to his arm like a bur to sheep's wool, but it seems I am mistaken. Old Somers calls out:

'Now for something a bit more old-fashioned, something the older folk can join in. We'll have "Black Nag".'

The couples sort themselves out in a minute. Harry and Will begin swaying and playing as if they have just awoke; all the other tunes are sleepy and droning compared to this – my feet are tapping when the master slips up behind me, claps his arm round my waist like a vice, and says: 'Now, Nan, thou canst dance "Black Nag" with me!'

Willy-nilly I am compelled, though I am not at all content.

Afterwards we have "A-hunting we will go". He gallops me so fast up and down the line I have no breath left to tell him what I think of him, roaring out the words above everyone else.

I am fairly ashamed.

> *'A-hunting we will go,*
> *A-hunting we will go,*
> *We'll catch a fox*
> *And put him in a box,*
> *And a-hunting we will go.*
> *Ta ra la, ta ra la, ta ra la,*
> *A-hunting we will go.'*

If I could free my hands, I would box my master's ears before all the world.

Olwen is sitting up with my mother. I find her asleep in the kitchen with her head on the table, and her long hair twining round the candlestick, all among the grease. Such a beautiful face I have never seen. I carry her up, lay her on my bed and take off her clothes. She wakes:

'Oh, Ann,' she says. 'Good night,' and sleeps again.

This morning Owen comes running to me: 'Come with me,' he cries. 'Tom would play with the scythe; he has cut his leg, and we have sent for the doctor to sew up the cut.' I find Tom very white, and the kitchen floor very red with his blood. Mrs. Somers is shrieking and sobbing; she wrings her hands and says it is his fault.

'Scythes are not to play with, but he would not be

warned. Oh, dear!'

I stop the bleeding with old towels and clean water until the doctor comes. He stitches it together.

'And who are you, my girl?'

'I am Shepherd's daughter from Cotterill's.'

'You! Well, you have done right. You would make a good nurse.'

Gabriel should be content to have a wife who can clean chimneys and stop bleeding.

Gabriel is coming to see me.

I am putting on a clean new calico cover on our book.

He rides so beautifully that I run down the hill to watch him come up the lane; I stand by the gate to wait for him, and truth to tell I am thirsty for the sight of him after so long. It seems so much time wasted to be stood there at midday doing nothing, so I tuck up my sleeves and stoop down to the brook to gather watercress for our tea.

There is my face staring back at me out of the brown water among the weeds, almost like a person drowned.

It looks so strange that for a minute I forget Gabriel, but I hear the horse and spring into the middle of the road. Gabriel shakes the whip at me, and calls my name loud; he jumps down, kisses me, and takes the horse by the bridle.

'Why, Ann, what have you? Your arms are wet and your feet all muddy. Sit on the gate, sweetheart, while I clean your shoes.'

I sit on the gate and he takes a handful of grass to wipe the mud away. We hear a step. Evan ap Evans passes; he scowls at Gabriel and says to me:

'Good day, love.'

'Who is that calling you dear names in Welsh, so friendly?'

'It is father's master, Evan ap Evans, and he is not friendly, but hard and sharp. He does that to vex me.'

'If he were not your father's master, I would show him!'

'I wish you could,' I says. 'Many a time I would have liked it!'

'Many a time?' he says. 'Many a time?'

Mrs. Somers is keeping my mother company. She is telling her how bad Tom's leg is, and how sure she is it is poisoned.

She is a very sad woman. We take this book out with us to the little spinney. Gabriel laughs when I show him the new cover. 'I hope the inside is as clean,' he says.

We are sat on a log among the bushes, and I see his face grown dark as he reads. At last he rises up and flings the book away with all his strength into the brambles and nettles.

'I know Welsh,' he cries, 'I understand why you looked on the ground when that man passed you, speaking his dirty tongue. Get away, you little bitch, and find your Welshman!'

'My friends are in that book. Pull it out of the brambles, Gabriel Ford, or I'll have no more to do with you.'

I take his arm and shake it. He pushes me on the ground. 'I'll take you from your Welshman and keep you from the parson!'

I twist away from him and run; he catches me, but I dash my hand into his face and scream, for his look is fearful. I run and run; when I can no more I sit down upon a stone and cry till my face is sore. I see him go riding down our lane, lashing his horse and galloping hard. I get up and at home I tell my mother Gabriel had to be gone early.

'He is a fine man,' says my mother, 'but I wish, Ann, you would not marry an Englishman. If you lived in Wales I could go perhaps to stay a bit with you. I would wish to die in my own country.'

In the dark I go out to the little spinney: my book is lying in the bushes, and I bring it home. It is mine now. Farewell, Gabriel.

I watch them wash the sheep before the shearing comes on. The poor things struggle on the edge of the pool, tramping up the mud.

The water is shallow and dirty, but in the middle it is still and very deep.

They are all round that bit of water in the shade: my father and Willy Preece are dipping with two young boys to help; the sheep are panting in the hurdles. I stand behind an elder bush that my father may not see me, and I hear the boys call Evan ap Evans a mean master.

'He works cripples on his farm because he can get them for less.'

'But he doesn't give them less work.'

'No, and they must put up with his curses.'

'No man dare stand up to him save Shepherd, and he is near as bad himself.'

'Never a shilling does he give his men at Christmas, nor Easter. Old Somers gives each man bacon and half-a-crown.'

'Old Somers is a fool. Which is richest?'

'Evans, curse him! Mean men make the money and

keep it. Come, shup. Come, shup, come, shup. Shepherd's ready for another pair.'

We have had a dreadful storm. I did not know it could be so bad here, where there are no hills worth speaking of to shut the lightning in.

I am on the way home from Salus, and I have to take shelter with the Somers; they are all in the kitchen watching the lightning.

'Now I do hope,' says Mrs. Somers, 'I do hope our Owen won't go sheltering under any trees.'

'Don't you fret, mother. Owen is no fool,' says her husband.

'But you never know, and fool or no fool is all the same with lightning, you are never safe from it. My uncle used to have a man on his farm – a full-grown man he was – who could only look after cows like a woman or help a little with the hay; no ploughing or harrowing or reaping. He had been struck by lightning when he was fifteen. In the leg it was.'

'But there's very few folk that *are*,' argues Mr. Somers, who should know better by now.

'And the lightning is so pretty, Mam,' says Chrissie, who wants to go outside and watch it from the gate.

'I don't know, and as for being pretty, my word, I think it is terrible, and smells awful they say.'

'Smells?' we all cry.

'That it does. I mind a dreadful storm once, oh, a very bad storm it was, but not so near as this, and a man I used to know when I was a girl went out with his brother to see if the cattle were safe. The lightning come down not fifty yards from them and burnt up a whole elm. They said it smelt awful. They were both big men, but they put their hands over their eyes and ran back to the house like children.'

'But I'm not affeared, Mam!' laughs Chrissie.

'Your great-grandfather said that,' says Mrs. Somers very solemnly.

'I like to watch it.'

'Your great-grandfather said that too. And one day when he was sat in the porch watching it, down it come like a blue serpent and got him in the arm! Just you take warning, Chrissie! He wouldn't, and it struck him three times until he stopped looking at it. I don't remember where he was struck each time, but there wasn't much left of him when I knew him. Your grandmother always put *her* head in the bread-pan, and it never got her.'

Chrissie begins to cry; Mrs. Somers does not heed, or perhaps she cannot hear, for she has stuffed both ears with jeweller's cotton at the beginning of the storm and sits looking at her feet.

'There's nothing to be affeared for,' says Mr. Somers. 'Don't take on, child.'

'And listen! There was another man my sister knew; he was hoeing turnips when the lightning come without any rain. He left his hoe and went into the garden because he was wise, but his cousin looked up at the sky and laughed, and *he* was struck. All they ever found was his buttons.'

'Oh dear,' says Chrissie, crying bitterly.

'I must go, the sun has come out,' I says.

'I never thought to see it again,' says Mrs. Somers, taking the wool out of her ears. 'Go and get the tea,

26

Chrissie. Whatever is the matter with the child? You will stay a bit, won't you, Ann? We don't see much of you, and it is so cheering to have a bit of talk.'

'Have you told her the news, mother?' asks Mr. Somers.

'No, fancy that! It went clean out of my head in the storm. Owen is going to his uncle's farm down at Monmouth next week. Oh, I do hope he hasn't been walking under any trees.'

'I hope he will be happy,' I says.

I wish I were.

Time is long in passing! I look at the clock and wonder how I shall get through tomorrow. My father asks me when I shall be married; I do not answer, and his look follows me.

Summer has come in: Mary's sheep will be up the mountains, and the master has begun to shear. Olwen comes over today. She puts her two hands to my face, turning it this way and that so that the light falls on it:

'Dear Ann,' she says, 'what have you?'

'Maybe I'm tired with the heat, Olwen.'

'Never. Tell me what has happened to you.'

She kneels down beside me.

'Gabriel and I have quarrelled. He has left me, Olwen; we shall not be married.'

She takes my two hands and lays her cheek upon them.

'He heard the master speaking Welsh to me, and thought he spoke too friendly. He is jealous of Evan ap Evans, that loves neither man, woman, nor beast.'

I take my father's dinner down to the big meadow,

where they are all shearing under the elms. Olwen is there, sitting on a hurdle swinging her legs, with her hair out of plait; so is young Williams's new wife. She comes from a town, and watches him as he shears with all her eyes. The master is stood close, too, looking and holding his watch in his hand; he scowls at Williams, who has made two cuts in five minutes.

'Look at him,' whispers Olwen; 'he is vexed, but he will not say so.'

'It is plain you don't know him,' I says. 'If he is vexed he will be out with the reason, and a double measure of cursing too.'

Olwen laughs out loud; the master looks up and sees us together.

'Good day,' he calls out, but he does not keep his eyes for long off the sheep that is struggling under Williams's shears. Suddenly he puts the watch back in his pocket. 'You need not come again, you are too slow.'

'Yes, sir,' says Williams, though he is not pleased. His wife puts out her tongue at the master as he turns away; she bends down to stroke her dog that sits by her quietly all the time, and I can see she is crying. I make to slip away when I see Evan ap Evans coming.

'Don't run away,' he says, 'I want to speak to thee.'

'I'm going back home. You cannot have anything to say to me.'

'But I have, and I will say it – leastways, I'll shout it if thou wilt not stay to listen. Olwen can go closer to watch them shearing; she cannot see very well from here, I know.'

'Not very well,' she says, and is off like a flash.

'Now, Ann, art thou vexed with me?'

'I've reason to be.'

He draws his brows together, as he does when he is angered.

'Thou art very saucy for a shepherd's daughter: very high and haughty thou art, Ann Goodman: had thy father not been such a good shepherd, thou mightst have had cause to rue it before now! But I am not here to quarrel. I'll ask thee a question. Wilt thou answer me straight like a man, since thou canst not speak to me like a woman?'

He fixes his eyes on me; I am not affeared at his black looks.

'Yes, I would like to answer you like a man if there were no folk here. But they might find it strange to see Evan ap Evans, farmer of Cotterill's, struck by a hired man's daughter!'

'What a tongue has our Nan!'

He walks a few steps from me, calling to the men to hurry. Suddenly he turns round:

'Answer me, or I'll bawl it for all the world to hear. Is it true that I have made trouble between thee and thy sweetheart?'

'Yes, you have done that.'

'How should that be? I am thy father's master, he is my shepherd, and how should I have anything to do with his daughter?'

'You called me your love when he was by. What right had you? He understood.'

He gives a kind of laugh, but I am nearer tears than I like for him to see.

'As good a right as any man!'

'No, no,' I cry.

'Well, I will not speak Welsh now. I thought it might seem homely to thee, thou being from the mountains, and it's a sweeter tongue than English.'

'No,' I tell him, 'I am English. I was with English folk in Wales, and I hate the Welsh and all their shifty ways of dealing. "Taffy was a Welshman, Taffy was a thief."'

'Ay, among Englishmen I'd cheat the log-heads out of every penny. Thou hatest the Welsh, dost thou? Is Myfanwy an English name?'

For once I cannot answer.

'I'll go to thy Gabriel.'

'You'll do no such thing. You've done enough.'

'I will. I will tell him that thou and I are nought but good enemies, and always have been. I shall tell him he is a fool – an English fool.'

'I'm going home,' I say. 'You cannot undo what you have done, even with your Welsh tongue.'

'I will, though,' shouts the master.

'Gabriel Ford will never take your word,' I answer back.

'Nor thine, or this would never have happened. How shalt thou marry him then? Ann, stay with me.'

'I'm going home,' I say again. 'I hate you, and if I could work you harm for what you have done, I would.'

I leave him standing stock-still; as I do I hear him whisper:

'There is a longing on me for my own country.'

I have looked for furious rage.

I go straight to Olwen.

'You are a strange friend, giving me away to the man I hate most in the world. Now tell me what you said to him.'

'Yes, I will. Only don't frown so, Ann.'

'When did you tell him?'

'I went to Cotterill's yesterday. I felt like Daniel in the lions' den!'

'Does anyone know beside the master?'

'No.'

Olwen tells me she ran off to Cotterill's the moment the baby was in bed.

'The yard was full of pigs, Ann, and when I opened the gate, because I could not climb over the spikes, a big sow ran out into the road. I run out after her, leaving the big gate open to drive her through; while I was chasing her, the rest came out and ran up the road the other way.'

She hears them squealing and grunting and thinks whatever shall she do, and which way shall she go? In the end she chases the sow as far as Baysham Marsh, where she turns her. As she comes up the lane, very hot and out of breath, she meets Miss Evans with her back hair falling down and her cap all crooked.

'What are you doing with my sow, child?' she asks, giving it a whack with her stick.

Olwen makes a curtsy.

'Please, Miss, she got out when I opened the gate. I come to see the master, and please the others are all gone up Hentland way.'

Olwen says Gwladys Evans goes up that lane like lightning, the sow galloping in front like a mad thing.

'Now pen her up, and come to help me with the others,

since you let them out.'

'I'm very sorry, Miss,' says Olwen; 'if you stand by the gate I think I can get them in.'

'My dear, do you think I want to stay here all night while you go catching pigs all over the parish? I have to go out, so come along.'

Olwen tells me she did want to laugh; Miss Evans looked very odd with her hair streaming behind her, scampering up the lane, hallooing and calling to the pigs, and asking questions all the time.

'You work for Mrs. Hill, don't you? When is Mr. Hill going to haul that elm trunk across my brother's hedge? Why have you come to see him? And what are you going to say? How old are you?'

Olwen says she is fourteen come next July.

'I'm sure you're not. You are much older.'

'No, I'm only that.'

'Nonsense, I know you are fifteen at least. Brenin Mawr! There's my pigs over in Scudamore's orchard! Whatever will he say? Creep through the hedge and drive them out quick, before they are seen. Here's a hole.'

As each pig comes through, Gwladys Evans gives it a whack.

'That's for leading me such a dance!'

Yet, Olwen says, she did not seem to be at all vexed.

'Well, now you had better come to the dairy and have a drink of milk. I am going out, so you shall sit in my kitchen and wait for the master. He'll be back in half an hour or so.'

She takes Olwen through the back door, gives her cake

and milk, and a bowl of gooseberries to top and tail.

'Put the tops and tails in the fire, and mind you don't throw any about; I cannot abide a dirty kitchen. And don't let the fire out.'

She puts on her bonnet, takes a shawl from the drawer, and goes out, leaving Olwen sitting there very contented. About an hour after, Olwen hears the outer dairy door bang; Evan ap Evans walks in whistling.

'Cythraul! What are you doing sitting here in the dusk? Are you a fairy?'

'Please, sir, I want to speak to you. I am Olwen Davies.'

'You are welcome,' says the master.

'Ann Goodman's sweetheart have left her because he heard you call her dear names in Welsh.'

She is almost frightened to death then, for he breaks out into his own tongue, which she cannot understand.

'What are you staring at?' he cries, after a while. 'What do you want?'

Olwen bursts out crying.

'I want to go home. I am affeared, I wish I hadn't come!'

'Come back,' the master calls, 'come back, Olwen, I've something to ask you. Come back, and I'll give you some cake and a whole duck!'

As Olwen tells me this, she puts her arm round me.

'I ran home, Ann, without another word. Are you still vexed with me?'

'Is that all?'

'Yes,' she says.

'Well, it's nothing but truth, though I hadn't thought to tell him.'

As I am stood in the kitchen, making a pudding, I hear my mother call out:

'Ann, wash your floury hands. The master is riding up the hill.'

'He won't come here, never fear,' I say.

She calls again:

'Quick! I can see him through the window; he is tying his horse to the gate.'

It is too late to wash; I have the door open for coolness, and the master is stood in it looking at me.

'Good day,' he says, 'I am riding into Wales, Ann Goodman. What message have you for your sweetheart?'

'None by you,' I answer.

There is something strange to me in his voice. He is speaking English. He flicks the lintel with his whip.

'Perhaps there'll be one to bring you.'

'If you are going to Gabriel Ford, I cannot stay you. But you are more likely to bring back a bruised face than any message.'

'Then you shall bathe it for me.'

I make no answer.

'Ffarwel, Nan. Time brings ointment to every hurt.'

He goes away. I wish we had never met!

My father says the master came home late last night. He has been away three days, and I have not heard his face was bruised.

I wish it had been!

He has brought no message.

34

I dream that I am in the kitchen at Twelve Poplars, sitting by the hearth. Mary touches me, she is stood close behind me.

'I can hear them coming, Ann,' she says.

I too hear the sound of wagon wheels. I run to the door: the master's heavy wagon is coming up slowly under the trees with my father on the front by Willy Preece. The wheels are dripping with water. They draw up before the door, and I see there is a coffin in the wagon, covered with a cloth. They carry it into the house.

What does this mean?

A month has passed. This evening on the way home from Salus I meet Mr. Hill, staring over the gate into the bottom field, where every man that can be hired round here is carrying the master's hay.

He turns to me.

'Gamus is still uncut. A heavy crop, Ann! Most of it is flat on the ground. The grass in the Oak Meadow has been lying out untouched this fortnight. My hay is ruined.'

'I've never known the weather so bad. Hay will be dear this year.'

'Evans will sell it dear! He has every man in the place. Oh, he can pay well when there's money to be made by it. He saves enough on his cripples to pay for his harvesting, while we who pay a fair wage all the year round see our crops rot. Curse him!'

'Yes, it is all in safe; this is the last field.'

'Mine is not fit for fodder. The Welsh hog!'

My father grunts when I tell him.

'Hill is too quick to mow, too slow to turn, too quick to carry. He has none to blame but himself.'

ANN'S BOOK

SECOND PART
1850

Gwyn ac oer yw marmor mynydd,
Gwyn ac oer yw ewyn nentydd,
Gwyn ac oer yw eira Berwyn,
Gwynnach oerach dwyfron Ann.

White and cold is the marble of the mountains,
White and cold is the foam of the rivers,
White and cold is the snow on Berwyn,
Whiter, colder is the breast of Ann.

ANN'S BOOK

SECOND PART
1850

My mother is dead.

I take my father his tea in the bottom meadow, where he is loading hay with the rest: when I come back there is my mother on the floor beside her bed, gasping for breath.

'What is it? What have you?' I cry, running to her.

'My heart!' she answers.

I lift her up in my arms and lay her on the bed. Her face is grey like ashes and damp with sweat; every minute her breath comes shorter, every minute it seems to me that she must die under my hands.

'Mae arnafeisian gweld John,' she gasps. 'I want to see John.' She has fallen into her own tongue, that she has not spoken since she was married.

There is no time to lose: from the window I can see my father down in the meadow, working by the gate. I lean out with my fingers to my mouth and give the shepherd's whistle; he looks up.

'Father!'

He throws down his fork. I wait but a moment to see him start on the way before going back to my mother, who is groaning.

'The pain, the pain,' she cries.

I sponge her face and lift her up. My father shouts from the kitchen to know what is wrong.

'Send Willy Preece for the doctor. I think Mother is dying,' I whisper down the stairs.

How long my father is away, and all the time my mother crying out to me to fetch him! But when he comes to her bed and tries to speak to her, she does not seem to know he is there.

'What is she saying? What does she want?'

'She is asking for you, Father.'

'Myfanwy, Myfanwy, I am here. Speak to her, Ann! Can't you? Speak her own tongue!'

'Father is here,' I tells her.

She grasps my wrists.

'Oh, be quick, Ann dear, be quick, I am dying.'

'He is here,' I cry over and over.

At last I tells my father to say:

'Rwaf yma wrtheich ymyl.'

He tries, word for word, after me, and she smiles as best she can.

'Will the doctor be long?'

'An hour may be, if he is in.'

'She will be gone before then,' I says.

There is nothing we can do to hinder her, but she is still alive when the doctor comes into the room. He looks at her once, and a minute after we see that she is dead. Without a word or another glance my father pulls the curtains and goes away downstairs.

'What was it?'

'Angina pectoris – her heart. Had she ever been at all like this before?'

'Never, but she has been ailing this past year.'

'Has she been crossed or thwarted today, or has she done anything different from her habit that might have upset her?'

'No, she has been in bed, knitting, like she always does.'

'Have you left her alone at all?'

'I was ten minutes gone to the field with my father's tea. She was well and smiling when I looked back at the window, waving her hand to me.'

He says that waving killed her.

After he has gone and it is quite dark, I go down to my father in the kitchen. He lights the candle and puts it on the table beside me with a piece of paper and a pen. 'Sit down here. Write to your cousin.'

'Not tonight, Father.'

'Yes – now. Tell her you will be going back to Wales, and Myfanwy too; it was a promise years gone by.'

I takes the pen in my hand.

'In the morning you must find a woman to help get her ready.'

I write: my father stands behind me, looking out of the window.

'I'll live alone,' he says.

In a while he goes up the stairs to my mother, and I hear the bolt thrust.

Parson comes and begins to talk about the funeral:

'She was too frail to attend the services, but of course she will be buried according to our rites and ceremonies?'

'Whose rites?' asks my father. 'Yours?'

'And yours,' says Parson sharply.

My father laughs.

'If rites are religious fancies, I leave them to other folk. Myfanwy had them: chapel and Wales was her wishes, and back over the Border she shall go, where she came from. I'll take her to Pentredwr, where I met her at a sheep fair, thirty years ago.'

This morning my father goes to the doctor for the certificate, and Mrs. Hill and Mrs. Somers come in to help me dress her. Gwladys Evans sends flowers from her garden. Mary comes over to fetch me. She goes up to my mother. 'Poor Myfanwy,' she says when she comes down, 'poor Myfanwy!'

My mother wears a long white shawl that I knitted for her in the spring to keep her warm in bed, and her face is younger than my memory of it. Mary and I walk to the bottom of the hill, where Morgan and the trap are waiting by the brook. The horse is fresh from standing; Cotterill's and our cottage are soon out of sight.

'Twelve Poplars is your home,' says Mary; 'your father is best left alone. My word, I could say something to him for making you write that letter with Myfanwy not cold, telling you to go the minute the breath is out of your mother's body!'

The master passes us, riding into Salus; he draws close in to my side.

'Art going back to the mountains for good, Ann?'

'I'm not coming back,' I answer, with my eyes on the horse's ears.

He looses the reins.

'Ffarwel, Ann.'

'Ffarwel,' I says.

Mary stares after him.

'Who is that man calling you by name? He was over at Tan y Bryn one evening when I was there.'

'It is the master.'

The dream comes true in every way: my father and Willy Preece bring my mother from England in a wagon. They are more than an hour late for the funeral, and three hours over the time we were all to meet at Twelve Poplars. After this wet summer the river is very hard to ford; the wagon is wet to the axles, and the black cloth over the coffin is dripping at the edges.

My father gets down.

'Don't carry her in, we're late as it is. We'll start away now. Are you ready?'

Willy Preece, Owen Somers, and Harry Edwards are the other bearers. They are all waiting, but Mary pushes them back.

'Myfanwy is coming over my doorstep if I have to carry her myself!'

They take my mother into the parlour, where there are

flowers for her; the curtains are drawn – my father will not wait above ten minutes, and for fear of trouble Mary gives in, though she sets her lips very tight.

It is a long way to the cemetery: Mary and I walk close behind the coffin, the rest follow us. We are the only kin, for my father would have none of our people at the funeral.

The minister reads:

'It is better to go to the house of mourning than to go to the house of feasting: for that is the end of all men; and the living will lay it to his heart. Sorrow is better than laughter: for by the sadness of the countenance the heart is made better.'

He prays that strength and consolation may be dealt to us.

The mountains are black with rain: when the coffin is in the grave, the storm breaks, and on the way back home we take shelter.

Mary has beer and food spread, but my father will not touch a morsel. She asks him to rest the night.

'No,' he says. 'I have no time to waste. Come into the kitchen, Ann.'

Mary's look follows us.

'See here, now your mother is dead I have no use for you; all you could do for me I could do a deal better for myself. You make trouble with the master, you would lose me my shepherding by your saucy ways. All the parish sees he is sweet with you; if you won't have him, stay here till his blood cools, but it is a fool of a woman that takes the man when she might have the master! Still, have it your own way, only don't you set foot over the Border without I sends for you. You will not be welcome. Maybe you could be useful later on when the lambing is on me.' He puts his hat on and turns away. Mary stops him in the doorway:

'What, you are never going back tonight?'

'I'm going to the Goat at Pentredwr. That's where I'll rest the night over.'

Mary begins to look sharp.

'Very well, Shepherd Goodman, go to your old Goat! But the horses don't stir from here tonight. They will be a deal more comfortable than you, I know. A bug-bitten man *you* will be tomorrow. Shall we see you in the morning?'

'No.'

'Well, let us be thankful for that! But I suppose you'll be over sometimes to keep an eye on your wife's grave?'

'Once I am out of Wales I stay out of Wales,' says my father.

'You are a worthless fellow, and the best thing a woman can wish you is that your sheep keep you so busy with foot-rot and maggots that you have no time to think of your own wickedness.'

My father goes out, banging the door. He shouts to Willy Preece through the window:

'Here you, swilling beer on a coffin, have the wagon down at the gate sharp at five.'

After an hour or so the folk go away, save those that are to sleep here. Owen Somers and Willy Preece go up into the granary to give the children rides on the trolleys. They have been sliding on the grain all the afternoon. Charlie drives the cows into the yard, and, going to the dairy, I take my milking stool and pail off the hook.

In the morning, just after we are astir, I see the empty wagon go up the hill with my father and Willy Preece on the front. They are sitting on the black cloth that covered my mother's coffin. I watch them go crawling out of sight, hoping that wagon will be the last I see of them this many a day.

Owen Somers comes to me in the dairy, where I am skimming the milk: I ask him to have some before he goes: he takes the cup from my hands.

'Shepherd says we shall not be seeing you this side of Christmas, Ann. Shall you be away all those months? Mother will miss you sadly.'

'It is no sorrow to me staying here, Owen; these parts are less strange to me than over the Border. Give my remembrances to your father and mother when you go home, and if you should see Olwen Davies, give her my dear love.'

'Yes, Ann. I will do that. Good-bye to you.'

Charlie and Georgie are holding his horse in the yard; he mounts and rides away, waving his hand to the children. My father would have no flowers on my mother's grave. Now that he is gone we carry roses and marigolds out of the garden to her. There are some bits of speedwell too, which Mary was used to tell me meant, 'God be with you.'

I am content to have my dairy to take my mind off other things.

Jenny is a strange child.

This evening she is sat in the kitchen window, holding the children's big Bible with the pictures open on her knees: beside her she has made a great pile of red and white rose petals. One by one she drops them between the pages.

'What are you doing, Jenny dear?'

'The red petals are for the happy pictures, and the white for the sad ones.'

She holds up the Bible for me to see: there is a white petal on the raising of Lazarus from the dead.

'But that surely is a happy picture. Lazarus was dead, and was called back to life again.'

Jenny shakes her head.

'No, it is a sad picture. Lazarus was asleep, and they woke him.'

Mary takes the children to church in the morning. I was used to go with them, but this Sunday I go to the Welsh service in the evening. There are very few folk, for most of the Welsh-speaking people are chapel. It is for fear of meeting Gabriel that I go this evening. He will never go where the Welsh tongue is spoken, so be that he can help it; he finds it bitter to work at Tan y Bryn, although it is a good place with a kind master. He was born and bred in England, and he has no use for the Welsh, nor for their way of speaking.

There is a cold wind blowing for July, and a deal of spoilt hay lying out in the fields. I look up Graig Ddu. Gwen Powys's sheep are wandering about, but Gabriel is not with them. After the service I go to the cemetery. Looking down upon my mother's grave, it seems strange to think of life at Cotterill's, and while I stand there lost, there is a footstep by the gate. It is Gabriel, staring at me through the bars; without a word I turn away, and he does not follow.

Mary asks me:

'Ann, what is wrong between you and Gabriel?'

'We have quarrelled.'

'Why?'

We are in the dairy, straining off the milk. I hold the muslin while she pours, and my hands tremble so that I let it slip.

'Careful,' says Mary. 'We'll have a bit of talk over this after we have done.'

Long as I have lived with her I would be more content to keep it to myself. But she must be told; everybody must notice that he has stopped coming here after me.

'What was the trouble?' she asks in the kitchen.

'Gabriel was jealous of Evan ap Evans, my father's master.'

'I fancy there are some things I could tell you about those two.'

'Yes, you said you were at Tan y Bryn the time the master come.'

'I was sitting in the kitchen with old Powys; Gwen and the girls were at Pentredwr. We had been having a lot of rain, and the spring had come through the floor again. There was the poor old man down on his hands and knees with a basin and saucer, saucering it up. When I come in at the door he threw them both against the wall, shouting:

'"Diawl! An hour have I been on my knees, and no more will I do. Ah, ah, ah, with the crickets singing round the fire and the water between the stones, indeed, it is unpeaceful even with Gwen away at the market."

'"I'll do a bit," I said. I had barely dipped up a saucerful when there came a knock on the door.'

Mary stops and looks at me very solemnly.

'It was the man that overtook us riding to Salus,' she says, 'a big dark Welshman and looks sour.'

'That's the master.'

'"Is Gabriel Ford a shepherd here?" he asked.

'"Yes, he is," we answered.

'"I want to see him."

'Old Powys told him he would have to climb Graig Ddu, unless he liked to wait until Gabriel came down to milk. Their sheep have had maggots badly this year, and Gabriel was up with them.

'"I will climb Graig Ddu," said your master.

'We asked him if he knew the way, but before we had finished pointing out the track Gabriel came into the yard; he had a bottle of Thorley's in his hand that he had been using on the sheep.

'"That is Gabriel Ford over yonder," I said.

'He went over at once: my word, Ann, you should have seen Gabriel's face when he saw your master coming!'

'I know well enough how he looked.'

'"There's going to be trouble; whatever can be amiss between those two?" I thought, seeing Gabriel's black scowl, and knowing him to be a stranger in these parts. I heard him ask in English:

'"Are you Gabriel Ford?"

'Gabriel answered:

'"I am, blast your soul!" and threw that bottle of Thorley's straight at your master's head: he ducked, but the bottle hit his shoulder and burst all over his coat. My word, Ann, that set things going!

'"Diawl!" your master yelled, and he caught Gabriel a

51

clip which sent him reeling through the stable door, though Gabriel dealt him a slash with his crook that marked him under his clothes, I know.'

'Did they harm each other?'

'Gabriel was hurt a bit, though not by the Welshman. That young mare they call Cadi was in the stable; whether she was frightened at Gabriel bumping in on her so sudden I cannot say, because I was right over by the kitchen door, only she kicked him out of the stable on to the muck heap in the yard, and for five minutes he was quiet enough – while we were throwing cold water over him. Your master went over very cool to the stream and washed off the Thorley's with his handkerchief; he got on his horse and rode off without another glance at us.

'Not very long after, Gwen Powys and the girls came back; they wanted to know why Gabriel had a black eye and a stiff leg, but he wouldn't say anything beyond the mare had kicked him. He went on with the milking as though nothing had happened, though everybody could tell he was in a boiling passion. Still, they were affeared to ask the reason, so to this day Gwen Powys is none the wiser.'

'Was that *all*? Didn't the master say why he had come?'

'Not a word to a soul, my dear. He just went off looking like murder.'

'He told me he would go to Gabriel and make him understand we were nought to each other.'

Mary looks up sharply.

'Then there was some cause for Gabriel to be jealous?'

'He heard the master calling me dear names in Welsh one day when he was come over to see me.'

'So your master *was* sweet with you! He is a fine man, Ann; it would be better for you than to marry a shepherd.'

'Those were my father's words to me just after we buried my mother. Listen, Mary. I hate Evan ap Evans!'

'Perhaps, seeing you were his shepherd's daughter – though you are as good as he is by blood and better by behaviour – he thought nothing of a kiss here and there.'

'There were no kisses.'

'Well,' says Mary, 'there is no telling what a Welshman means by what he says.'

And she calls the children in to their supper. I do not answer, for sometimes, since I have left Cotterill's, I have thought the master loved me.

When we are sat sewing in the porch, there comes a bang on the back door: it is a man in a black velvet coat and plaid trousers, with a jug in one hand and a gridiron in the other.

'What do you want?' says Mary.

'I am selling china and hardware.'

'Well, if that is all your stock you will soon be sold out. Good afternoon to you.'

She begins to shut the door, but he does not move off the step.

'Ah, it is good to hear English again! The folk here have a tongue that we cannot understand, me and my little girl out there.'

We look past him into the yard, where we see a little donkey-cart and a child sucking an apple among a crowd of pots and pans.

'What else do you sell?'

'Brushes and buckets, funeral cards and syrups.'

'Syrups!' cried Mary. 'Have you any cough cures?'

He pulls a bottle out of his pocket.

'This mixture will cure any cough in a week. Not one of those railway-train cures, but a good steady reliable brew.'

'How much is the bottle?'

'One shilling and sixpence. Give a teaspoonful after every cough, and mix it with water to make it last – it is very strong.'

'Is it too strong for a little girl?'

'Oh, no, no, no. Bless you, no! It is the mixture I always give my own little girl out there.'

Mary buys the mixture and a scrubbing brush. Ten minutes after he is gone, Margiad Powys runs into the kitchen all out of breath.

'Has a man selling china been to you?'

'Yes. He was here but a few minutes since.'

'Cythraul! Which way did he go?'

'Oh, up the hill.'

'Oh, it is too hot to run up there after him.'

'Why, what is it?' I ask.

'He has stolen a drench Gabriel had for Cadi. He told mother how happy he was to be among his own people again, and asked her who won the prize for singing at the Eisteddfod this year. While she was gone to ask he must have put it in his pocket. It was on the table by the door.'

Mary and I give a look at each other; she takes the bottle of cough mixture off the dresser and hands it to Margiad.

'The Welsh varmint!' she says.

How slowly the days go by without Gabriel coming to see me in the evenings and walk with me to church on Sundays. In England there was my mother to look to, and the master to vex and plague me; at Cotterill's I was not used to meet him in the fields like I was here, where we both grew up.

Yesterday, crossing the bridge, I see him fishing in the pool where I was used to go with him and vex him by throwing my fish back. He does not see me leaning on the bridge, watching him as he watched me through the gate.

This morning the sun comes out. We gather up all the dirty clothes and make a washing day of it, putting off the churning till tomorrow.

Mary calls Charlie to her.

'Here, come and get the copper ready. Mind you fill it up to the brim and then be off to play with Georgie and Jenny. Mind now what I am telling you, and keep them out of mischief.'

Charlie is a good-hearted boy but stupid; in the wash-house we find the copper filled but the fire unlit – we lose half an hour waiting for the water to boil. It is a big wash for two wet weeks: there are sheets and towels and blankets.

'I'll wash; you rinse and wring,' says Mary.

We spread the things to dry over the blackberry bushes in the orchard, where it is sunny.

Jenny comes in crying just before dinner.

'I feel sick, Mam.'

'What have you been eating?'

'Apples, Mam,' says Jenny, sobbing and crying.

'Apples! They're as green as gooseberries. Who gave them to you?'

'Charlie did, to keep me out of mischief while he played up the tree with Georgie.'

Mary carries her off to dose her well.

'Run down to the orchard, Ann, and see what those boys are up to,' she says.

They are up the big tree playing sailors. One of our clean sheets is tied to a branch for a sail, flapping and torn, and George is waving one of his shirts tied to a stick by both arms.

Mary and I are very angry; Charlie has to go with bread for his dinner, and Georgie has to learn his duty to his neighbour. And we have to boil the sheet again and sew up the rents.

At sundown I pass through the Winllan on my way home from the cemetery. Gabriel is there, splitting logs, with Cadi and a cart; so we meet face to face alone, and I can see he is my sweetheart still.

Without a word spoken I stand beside him, watching his dark face and the mallet falling on the wedge. It is deep in the wood when there is a crack, the mallet head flies past my ear, and strikes against a tree behind me.

Gabriel drops the shaft, staring, and catches me in his arms.

'Forgive me, Ann; it was in my heart to hurt you! The head was coming loose with every blow, and yet I would not tell you.'

'I saw it, but I would not move for pride.'

He stoops to kiss my mouth: I push him off.

'Loose me,' I cry.

'Is your father's master sweet with you?'

'You would not take my word,' I says slowly in Welsh.

Gabriel scowls at the tongue.

'Loose me.'

He lets me go on my way; a field beyond I hear the rumble of the cart behind me, and turn my head: Gabriel comes up with me, he stretches out his hand; I take it, set my foot on the shaft, and stand up beside him. He keeps me steady with an arm round my waist.

Mary sees us come into the yard.

'What happened?' she asks me when we are going to bed. I tell her.

'Ah, everything comes right in the end,' she says, very content.

Our two black cows are sold at Pentredwr fair. Gabriel goes with Megan and Margiad against his will, because they have to leave before the fighting begins. Afterwards he comes to me.

'They pestered me to take them and buy them coloured handkerchiefs. I would have nought to say to them, but these are for you.'

He gives me sweets in a box.

'Ann, what makes you look so different these days? What have you been doing to yourself? Is it your black frock?'

'A deal of sad things have happened since you left me, but it was you and the master worked this with me.'

'Curse him!'

'All the world does that.'

'Then there must be good reason for it. When will you marry me – when the mourning is done?'

'It is too soon to talk of that,' I says.

While Gabriel and the girls are gone to the fair we go with Gwen Powys gathering whinberries up Graig Ddu. Gwen looks at her sheep.

'It's terrible to see them so lame and ailing. This has been a bad year: no fruit, all the hay lost, and by the looks of it the corn harvest may go the same way.'

Mary looks very grave.

By midday we have all filled our baskets – Jenny's mouth is purple with juice, and she cannot eat her dinner. Just after we have finished the rain comes down like a flood and we are soaked to the bone long before we can reach the house. On the way down I fall, cutting my knee, and Jenny cries out at the sight of the blood, so that a person would think it was her own.

We have to give Gwen Powys all dry clothes, and when we put hers on the horse before the fire we cannot help but see that she goes with only two petticoats – a grey flannel and a pink cotton.

'Saves the washing,' she says, seeing our surprise, that we cannot hide.

'One day she will take to wearing gloves to save her fingers,' Mary whispers.

We make our whinberries into jam and two tarts; Gwen Powys tries to take more than her share.

In the evenings Gabriel comes to see me.

But it is not like old times together.

While I am in the dairy churning, Charlie passes the window as idle as a plough-boy in August. The butter has just come, and I am letting off the buttermilk.

'Charlie, fetch me a bucket of water,' I say.

He takes the bucket I hand him through the window.

'Shall I put it in the churn?'

'Yes,' I tells him, pouring the buttermilk into the pig-trough with my back turned.

When I look round there is a stream coming out of the churn; Charlie has put in boiling water from the copper, and though I rush to take out the bung, half the butter is melted.

Mary says Charlie must go. Last night the fox come and killed five ducks, because he forgot to shut them up.

The weather has come in hot and fine.

Gabriel goes to church with me this Sunday. Afterwards we walk on to my mother's grave with honeysuckle that we gather in the hedges. She was used to call it fairy's fingers.

Gabriel says, 'Will you marry me in the spring, Ann?'

I cannot answer.

Sian Pritchard from Glanrafon is married to Abel Daw in the chapel at Pentredwr today. He keeps a draper's shop in Salus. Her father is fair furious at the marriage, being a true Welshman that would have his daughter marry one of her own country, but her English mother is well content the girl should go back over the Border.

Five years ago this July, Abel comes to Glanrafon in the evening with a pack on his shoulders as a journeyman. Mrs. Pritchard was that overjoyed to make welcome one of her own country that she kept him the night over, and by candle-light he and Sian cast such looks at each other as they neither of them ever forgot. The next year Abel came again to ask Sian if she would be his wife, and she said she would. He had started his shop, but when her father came to hear of it he fell into a rage, and went at Abel with a flail before Sian, till he was all but dead had she not dropped down in a fit on the threshing floor. She was so mortal ill that her father swore he would never thwart her or cross her again, so be she got better. For years Abel never come near her; at last she sent him a letter, and now for his promise Mr. Pritchard must put up with the wedding.

These last evenings I have been making her lace for a present. Mary went to the chapel; she said the lace was sewn on the wedding dress.

When the sun is down and the day cools off towards nightfall, Gabriel and I go up to Graig Ddu. He has his dog and his crook with him, and in his hand is a bottle of Thorley's, which makes me think of the master.

'Ben is in for the trials at Pentredwr. You'll be coming, Ann? It's not like a celebration,' says he.

'Yes. I'll be there.'

'You shall see us win the cup from the Caernarvonshire bitch.'

We stop at the pool where we was used to catch trout.

'Could you catch them in your hands now?' he asks.

It is already dusk when we are among the sheep. Ben fetches them together in the hollow called the Basin, and Gabriel and I sit down on a rock and wait for the moon to rise.

'Gwen Powys gives me but a scrap of candle for the lantern, so when there is free light I use it. She is the nearest woman in these parts, and many of them are near enough, God knows! She stints for food and light and firing.

She keeps a sharp eye on the almanac too, and at full moon my candle is shorter by an inch, be the weather fair or foul. The mountain is well named Graig Ddu. I have been up and down these paths on some dark nights, Ann.'

'Have you seen the Roman soldiers marching through Craig Dinas and the White Lady that drowned herself in Llyn-tro?'

'Never, and I have fished it many a night alone. All I heard was an otter splashing off the bank. It's a lonely place after dark under those trees, with the water rushing over the stones. There's never hardly much of a moon down there.'

I cannot see his face, but his voice changes after a moment. He points down where we came from.

'There are no lights in Tan y Bryn, you see? Gwen Powys sits by the hearth knitting stockings in the dark to save candles, and if Megan and Margiad are not out visiting or courting, they have to go to bed. It's well for them they are handsome girls.'

'You speak discontented, Gabriel' I says, thinking he has good reason for it.

'I have worked here fifteen years, and now I have done with Wales – done with it. Come spring we will be married. Perhaps I can find a place over the Border, where candle-ends count for less. Ah! if I can win the trials.'

He sits there silent with his arm round my waist.

'Look,' I say, 'the moon is up, we can count the sheep.'

'There's all the night before us. Now I can see you, Ann. How beautiful you are!'

He takes the pins from my hair and pulls it round my shoulders. I struggle to be free of him, but he holds me fast.

'Light the lantern for me, Gabriel, and let me go.'

He scowls.

'You love that Welshman! Time was when you could bear to be beside me half an hour without whining to be off.'

'Time never was when I would sit on the mountain till midnight. Loose me, I tell you.'

'We are doing no wrong here together,' says Gabriel angrily.

I am affeared. Suddenly I loose his arm and run from him down the path. He comes away after me, then stays at the edge of the Basin shouting and cursing.

In my heart I know now that we shall never marry.

August has come in hot and cloudy.

Early in the morning, before the others are awake, I go out mushrooming. It is not very long before I know someone has been through the meadows: there are footmarks in the dew and no rabbits feeding. And the home meadow is bare of mushrooms where last night I marked many for the picking. In the lower pastures I see a woman, thin as a crow, stooping with a basket in her hand.

'Good morning, Miss Powys,' I says behind her. 'What are you doing taking my cousin's mushrooms?'

Gwen Powys almost lets the basket fall in her fright. 'I came out early to gather them for a little surprise to Mrs. Maddocks, and it was in my mind to leave them on the doorstep,' she gabbles.

Margiad's head is bobbing above the hedgerow as she stoops and raises herself; Gwen's eyes go roving round the field while she is speaking.

'It was very kind of you. Myself, I haven't had the luck to

find a mushroom. You have sharp eyes, Miss Powys, but thank you all the same. I'll take the mushrooms with me to save you the walk.'

And I goes off with my basket full of her gathering.

August is a bad month for beasts; our cows have been very vexing lately, kicking and wasting the milk. This evening our only Welsh Black kicks me when I am milking the shorthorn next her; she strikes the leg off the stool and drenches me with the milk.

Morgan comes running, thinking to find me on the way to death from a blow in the back, but the stool takes the most hurt, and the cow too, when he beats her for her hastiness. There is a black bruise on my leg which I shall feel for many a day to come. And when I loose them from the chains, the blue cow that Mary brought up by hand like a child, spoilt and petted, goes to horn me, and only Morgan going at her with a pitch-fork saves me from a hole in the thigh.

Gabriel was used to say kind words drive a cow beside her senses: they must always be used to hard ways and the whip. Every evening he is in the Lower Pastures, training his dog for the trials. Save only my father, he is the best shepherd known to me in England or Wales. His ways are quicker, but as yet he lacks the patience my father keeps only for his sheep. When Ben has finished work, Gabriel comes over to me. He shows me a red mark under his ear like a sore place, and tells me how he come by it. Last night the rain come through the roof on to his bed, so that he woke to find himself wet and shivering; he got up to dry himself in front of the embers in the kitchen, and while he was at it he fell asleep on the settle. Early, before it was light, he woke again with a weight on his shoulders and breast: it was Gwen's sandy tom-cat curled up by his head, licking the skin over the great vein in his neck so that he might suck the blood. He was almost through when Gabriel thrust him off.

It seems it is never wise to sleep with a cat in the room, for their natures are as savage and bloodthirsty as any tiger's.

I take Jenny and Georgie down to the sheep-wash to bathe. For a time they are very good, till Georgie slips out through the hurdles, chasing a fish, and finds the river too strong for his little legs; it catches him up before he can grasp the hurdles, turns him round and round, and away he goes, kicking and rolling over among the rocks, sometimes on his face and sometimes on his back, till the current carries him screaming and half-drowned into Llyn-tro, where the water turns on itself like a wheel and is very deep. Before I have the wits to do anything, Charlie runs past me like a flash; he jumps into the pool without a stop, boots and all, and drags Georgie to the side by his hair: I give him my hand, and in a minute they are up the bank and out of the quiet black water, that has such an evil look, even by day, that the folk hereabouts shun it, for all the fine fish in it, save Gabriel, who has no fear of spirits, and swims like the salmon-trout he catches there.

For my part, I cannot see deep water, running or still, without a shiver, like some harm will come to me from it, and the sight and sound of a waterfall is full of terror.

Now I cannot forget that if Charlie had not saved Georgie, I would never have done it.

His teeth are clicking with fear and cold. We wrap him in the children's clothes and my apron.

'Come back to the farm with me, Charlie,' I say, 'the mistress shall know what you have done.'

Charlie shakes his head.

'No, I am affeared.'

'Affeared? Have you been up to something? She'll forgive you. She'll want to thank you, Charlie.'

But nothing will move Charlie, and we have to leave him, streaming with water, on the river bank.

Back at the house Mary and I put Georgie to bed in blankets and hot bricks to his feet.

'What!' cries Mary when I tell her, 'Charlie pulled him out? Oh, Ann, I had sent the boy off home not a minute before and told him never to set his foot on my doorstep again, because not half an hour ago I told him to throw the stale buttermilk into the pigs' trough, and he went and poured away all this morning's milk, though I *said* the red crock, and the milk was in a yellow one. Dear, dear, and now he has been in the river after our Georgie! There's something in having an English boy about the place, even if he is thick-headed. A Welshman never would have gone in the river after the child.'

'You mistake the Welsh, that's plain,' I say; 'they are a brave foolhardy lot, too apt at running into danger for no purpose at all. I have been told that father's master, Evan ap Evans, went into the river when it was in flood after a sheep, and this river here is but a runlet to ours at its lowest.'

'A sheep, yes. A sheep's worth money. Mark my words, he would never have gone in after a little boy.'

I laugh out loud: Mary looks at me sharply and smiles:

'But there, opinions differ,' she says, 'and lately I have been seeing your mother's blood in you, Ann – all that is good in it. Put on your bonnet, there's a good soul, and go down to Charlie's: tell him I am more than thankful to him, poor boy, and, from this day on, it is little scolding he will get at Twelve Poplars. Bring him back with you, for if he's a fool he's a brave one.'

Charlie is sitting in his mother's doorway dressed in his Sunday clothes and eating his dinner with brown paper pinned over him to keep off the gravy. When I tell him Mary's words, he gets up with a smile, puts the bowl on the table, kisses the cat, and makes ready to follow me, brown paper and all.

Something possesses Gwen Powys to ask Mary and me to take supper at Tan y Bryn, and so that we may have a laugh together afterwards we say we will go. When we get there, we find she has a party of Welsh friends there, and at supper theirs is the tongue spoken. Mary looks quite pleasant, though at heart she is like Gabriel in thinking it strange that the folk here should prefer their own tongue to English, but Gabriel sits at the bottom of the table glowering on the company.

Gwen has put out her blackberry wine; it sets the men to singing reckless words from 'Men of Harlech', despite his mutters and angry looks.

One of them jumps up from his place shouting:

'I drink to Wales!'

Gabriel roars:

'And I to England!' and stands facing the other across the table. Megan and Margiad clap their hands; Mary looks serious.

'There'll be trouble in a minute, the men are hot as coals,' she whispers.

Gwen purses up her lips.

'I give the Border,' she says, very quiet.

We all drink it down, and for once Mary and I have to forgo our laugh.

Gabriel hears me singing in the fields.

'Why do you sing in Welsh?'

'It is sweet for singing.'

'What was that sad song?'

'An old one I heard a man sing months ago.'

'It was your father's master sang it?'

'Yes, at a May dance.'

'Do you love that Welshman?'

'No.'

'When I hear you speak of him I tremble with rage.'

'You have no need,' I says; 'one day your temper will work you harm.'

'Do you love me?'

'*No.*' I answer him from my heart.

He draws in his breath and leaves my side.

Gabriel has taken up with Margiad: three times they walk slowly up and down beneath the poplars.

For years she has hated me for his sake.

67

Pentredwr is full of shepherds and their masters come for the trials tomorrow: there are English and South Welsh besides those from hereabouts, and some, they say, come all the way from Cumberland.

Two cows calved this week, so I take twelve pounds of butter to Mrs. Williams at the Goat. In the yard there are traps and carts of all sorts and colours; among them I see one high yellow two-wheeled cart with a liver-chestnut mare between the shafts that I have reason to know, and the lettering is plain, even from the other side of the road:

Evan Evans,
Cotterill's Farm, Salus.

My father comes down the street with the master's dog, Twm, at his heels. He takes hold of the mare's bridle and leads her off to the stables without seeing me watching him from the window.

The master has come to the trials!

Gabriel waylays me in the market-place.

'Did you mean what you said the other night in the meadows?'

I pull my arm from him, for I will not bear with his rough ways.

'Yes, I did. With all my soul.'

'You will not have me for your sweetheart?'

'I have done with sweethearts.'

He keeps pace with me, ranting and storming under his breath, till on a sudden he falls silent; across the street Evan ap Evans is walking slowly up and down, and

Gabriel's eyes follow him.

The trials are held on the lower slopes of the mountains beyond Pentredwr; Mary and I go over in the afternoon, when the novices are out of the way.

It is days that Gabriel has not been near me. He is stood over among the shepherds, with Ben on a chain, the only English sheepdog there, and I think to myself that he will not be able to pick me out of the crowd; but I am mistaken: he turns his head, fastening his eyes on my face with all his black rage behind the look.

'Do you see who is there, Ann?' Mary says, taking hold of my arm between her finger and thumb. She points to my father, stood a little away from the others with Twm; beside him is the master, poking his head forward as he talks. He waves his stick and my father spits.

'Well, he is a hard unnatural man serving a ruffianly master,' whispers Mary. 'Just look at the pair of them quarrelling and disputing over there in the sight of all the world. They might settle their differences before they come among decent quiet folk.'

By the looks of it they are still at odds when the trials begin, but when the first dog is off up the field, the master folds his arms and watches as though his life hangs on it.

The sheep are loosed three at a time from the higher meadow: there are two of them and a this year's lamb as wild as they can find them. The dogs must bring them down towards the shepherd who stands by the judges' box, through a gap in the hedge into the meadow, where all the world is stood blaming and praising the man for his handling of the dog.

There are four trials before the penning, which is the hardest to do: the sheep are driven between two hurdles, turned and driven back through two more, turned again through a gate from left to right, and once more through another gate from right to left. The shepherd may not move a pace until his dog has been through all four, but both must do the penning, and it's strange to see that more often than not it is the shepherd that is at fault. Only seven minutes are given at Pentredwr for all the work, beginning to end.

There are half a dozen turns before the Caernarvonshire bitch that has been first in the trials all over Wales. Some of them work well, but none under time, while she has them penned with half a minute to spare. She works without a fault; once the sheep break, but she turns them before much harm is done, and I can see Gabriel never takes his eyes off her.

'He'll find that hard to beat!' cries Mary. 'More's the pity. My word, I would like to see an Englishman win – so be that it isn't John Goodman, with all respect to his daughter.'

'But the master's Welsh,' I says, 'and the dog is his.'

When it comes to Gabriel, there is a hush in the crowd, for folk are beginning to know him, and Ben works faster than I have ever seen him. In four minutes they are up with the pen, though the sheep are wild and like to break with the rushing; Gabriel comes down with a run, and we think it is all over when the lamb breaks. Ben is off up the field like a flash, he turns it before it gets to the boundary, and the two of them come down full tilt to Gabriel, who turns the lamb in its rush straight into the pen with a wave of the crook.

Everybody bursts out cheering. Mary is smiling all over her face.

'Half a minute less than the bitch. There's a bit of work for you! Now we shall see what your father can do; his master looks black as the inside of a cow.' Indeed he does, and well he may.

'My father is not used to the ways of the mountain sheep; he is a proper English shepherd that takes his time, and the master must be mad to give him leave to put Twm in for the trials.'

'Things are the other way, I think,' says Mary, staring at my father that walks slowly to his place, cleaning his nose.

It seems I am right, and my father shows no knowledge of these sheep; he lets Twm go too far on the first drive, and they rush over the boundary in a panic. The judge blows his whistle.

'Another trial!' shouts Evan ap Evans above the laughing. My father throws down his crook cursing, and the master shakes his fist at him. I see Gabriel grinning, and it makes me fairly angry.

'Another trial!' I bursts out without a second thought that I am a fool.

'Ann, I am ashamed of you!' cries Mary, taking hold of me by the arm.

'Another trial! another trial!' the master yells, getting a sight of me.

'I'll be damned if I'll do it,' my father shouts so that all the world can hear. And he walks off with Twm.

Gabriel wins the cup, and I wish him joy of it.

71

This evening I do the milking alone; the cowshed door stands open, and with my head in the cow's flank I can hear nothing but the milk spurting into the bucket. When I look up I nearly loose it in my surprise, for there is the master stood beside me, smiling down like he was used to over the garden wall in the spring.

'Good day, Ann Goodman. Did you laugh at me at the trials?'

I say nothing.

'As high as ever!' he mutters. 'Gabriel Ford will be in a glory now he has won the silver cup.'

'Yes, indeed, I am glad he won it. What made you put Twm in the trials?'

'The devil take you!' shouts the master.

The cow flicks her tail across my face, stinging like a whip and drawing the tears to my eyes; the master holds it while I milk her dry: she does not like it and tries to kick.

'The milk will all be wasted; I wish you would go,' I says, nearer to tears than I can understand.

'I have news for you from Olwen Davies.'

I will not ask him his news, and he bends over me looking into my face.

'Come, Ann, look up. Give me a sight of you to take back to England with me. I am not speaking Welsh, though indeed it is on the end of my tongue, cariad.'

I look up.

'What is the news?'

'Olwen sends you her dear love, and for that matter there could be no better man to carry it than myself —'

The iron bar falls into the socket with a crash; the door is fast, and Gabriel is stood inside it.

He says nothing; nor does the master: like two bulls they come together and I cannot stay them. There is blood on their mouths and running down their chins; their breath comes panting, their eyes are red. Charlie bangs on the door, the cows fling themselves from side to side, pulling at their chains.

My knees grow weak at the sight. I am affeared of them as I have never been when they have turned on me.

'Stop, stop!' I cry, almost out of my senses. 'Master – Gabriel, I cannot bear it!'

It is only a matter of moments: the master knocks Gabriel against the wall; he falls on his knees, then full length, and there is blood among his hair.

'Is he dead?'

'No, beaten. Cymru am byth!' The master laughs.

'Then open the door and let in some air.'

Charlie and the master carry him into the house; he has a great cut in the head, long, but not deep, and his face is swollen and black. As I follow them from the cowhouse, I see the silver cup lying among the straw with a dent in its side: they have trodden on it and twisted the stem. Charlie rides into Pentredwr for a doctor, but long before he returns, saying he cannot find the house, Gabriel is sitting up on the settle with a piece of old pillowslip round his head. Mary is looking to him; I let her, for I never want to speak to him or touch him again.

The master is holding his head under the pump in the yard; his lip is cut and one eye is quite shut. I bathe it, I wipe his face.

'Ann, how thou didst cry!' he whispers.

I brush the dust and straw from his coat, and bring him buttermilk to drink. The silver cup comes first to my hand from my pocket where I have kept it. At first I throw it down, then pick it up and fill it to the brim. The master takes it, and my hand.

'Cariad, have I won the cup after all?'

'Drink,' I answer, 'and never come here again. I wish one of us three were dead!'

Mary calls me down to see Gabriel.

'Will you come, Ann?'

'Yes, this time, but never again,' I says, my mind fixed to end it.

He is waiting for me in the threshing-room, and his face is still a painful sight.

I go up to him.

'Say what you want to say, and be done with it, for this is the last time I'll hold talk with you, so be that I can help it.'

'Are you going to marry me, Ann?' he asks, twisting the flail in his fingers like a snake.

'Never in the world, Gabriel!'

'Are you going to marry your father's master?'

'Who gave you leave to question me?' I bursts out in my rage and shame, 'you who look no farther than the doorstep for a woman to take the place you swore was mine until we both should die!'

'There never was another woman in that place, and there never will be.'

'Margiad?'

'Margiad means nought to me.'

'More shame to you then that you took up with her; you and the master have made me look a fine fool before folk with your fighting and brawling. Between the two of you you make my life a misery, and then you talk of marriage! Leave me alone; I hate both of you!'

'So that you hate him I'll leave him content till you come round to my way of thinking.'

'If you are an Englishman, Gabriel Ford, then from this day I'll count myself as Welsh. You are a jealous, unreasonable man, and I pity the woman your choice falls on!'

'You'll have need to.'

'You look now ripe for murder. Go away and never trouble me again.'

For a minute it seems that he will strike at me with the flail. Throwing it down, he swallows his rage and seizes my wrists so that I cannot pull them away; stooping, he kisses me, and loosing me, leaves me standing half choked with rage.

Mary comes in to me with a cup of tea.

'Here, drink this. My word, Ann, you are well rid of that devil! I could hear him bellowing right over in the dairy. In your place I should keep clear of Gabriel Ford.'

The countryside is full of talk; it is well for me my mourning keeps me close at home.

The other day Gwen Powys comes over to ask me why Gabriel's silver cup that he won at the trials is dented; people say he and the master fought for it.

'There might be something in it – you never know. I

75

wonder,' she says while her sharp eye wanders round. We are vexed and not over polite.

A day or two after Mrs. Pritchard walks all the way from Glanrafon to ask if there is a charge against the master, and when she has drunk three cups of tea Mary sends her off none the wiser but for the recipe which she wanted as an excuse for her visit.

The minister cannot come himself among the church folk that he has said are going to hell; he asks Jenny questions which she is far too young to understand.

'Ask Cousin Ann,' she says; but when he meets me he looks the other way.

One afternoon, when I am at the cemetery, Mr. Davies comes to see me. He has been first to Twelve Poplars, and Mary, busy with the baking, tells him where to find me.

He fetches water from the stream to fill the jars, then he puts the flowers in. He talks in a harsh way that used to put me in mind of a raven when I was a child, but his words are kind enough.

'For fifteen years you have been coming to my church, and I remember well the summer you spent at Twelve Poplars long before you lived there. If you are troubled, Ann, and I can be of any help to you, come to me and think of me as your friend.'

Mr. Davies is an old bachelor, and for all I think well of him, I cannot tell him my heart. I thank him for his kindness; he sighs, and on the way home talks of the coming harvest.

A sight that is strange in my eyes is the hay lying out black and rotten in the fields while the corn stands ripe and ready to the harvest. Scythes are coming off the walls, and men are waiting for the hiring.

I wake in the night to find a red light shining through my window on the foot of my bed, clear enough for me to see my clothes on the chair.

I get up, and outside the door Mary calls that a rick has fired at Tan y Bryn, and she has sent Morgan off to lend a hand.

We watch the fire from her bedroom till the dawn puts out the glow in the sky. Mr. Powys was always one to gather his hay too soon; this way he has lost it as surely as Mary, whose crop is lying out in the fields.

'Well,' she says, putting on her clothes as sharp as if she had slept all night, 'this will give Gwen something new to talk about!'

I see Margiad alone in Pentredwr, looking as miserable as a moulting hen.

Today we bake bread pies and tarts that we may go a week without cooking.

Mary has hired five men for the harvesting; they will do the mowing and we shall do the binding ourselves, all because the weather looks too bad to put it off any longer. Mary goes to see Mrs. Williams at the Goat, whose son died last week of consumption, and I tidy up the kitchen after our cooking. With the day so warm and fine I let the fire out and boil up the big kettle for tea under the copper. After my wash I think there will be a tidy place for me to sit sewing, but when I come down I find ashes on the hearth, the flagstones black with soot, and the embers raked out of the grate all over the floor. What is worse, a draught from the window to the open door has blown ash-dust on everything.

I hear the pump going in the yard, and there I catch Jenny and Georgie, smeared like chimney-sweeps, pumping and pouring water over Charlie, that is blacker by far than either of them, and soaking wet into the bargain.

'What have you been doing now?' I cry. 'It seems I cannot turn my back a minute!'

'Georgie says the swallows live up the chimney in the winter, and Charlie went to have a look at their nests,' says Jenny, half laughing and half crying.

'Then Charlie can go straight in and sweep up the kitchen after he has cleaned himself.'

'And what will happen to Georgie?'

'I shall tan him well with my shoe for talking nonsense.'

'And what will you do to me?'

'Wash your face with soap and give you a clean pinafore.'

They all burst into howls, and I am forced to give them bread and treacle before they will stop. Mary comes in while I am on my hands and knees scrubbing the floor.

'We shall have to keep Charlie, I suppose, but oh, I could wish it had been another body pulled Georgie out of the water!'

The harvest has begun.

From morning till evening we are hard at it in the wake of the mowers, gathering up the swathes, binding them, and making them into sheaves because we are pressed for time. There is no sun to scorch our necks, but our backs

ache enough to kill us with the stooping.

My place is behind Twm Williams; he never seems to tire, though he mows the widest swathe of all.

Towards sun-down we cannot hold ourselves up for very weariness.

'Enough; if it must spoil, it must,' says Mary. We go in to supper: she is half asleep and I can hardly drag my feet. Even in bed our bones ache, and in the night we hear rain falling.

The barley is stood near a fortnight in the field with not a chance of drying. After a fine day comes a wet one; twice there are heavy showers in the night. Thank heaven we have no oats!

Gwen Powys comes over to talk a bit, bringing some stockings to knit. She uses such hard coarse wool that we are all very sorry for her poor brother, it must be like walking in canvas.

'I buy my wool for wear and not for show. Who sees Trefor's feet? And I knit very tight to make the wool go a long way.'

One day she will take to knitting his stockings out of binding twine, for I see her looking very hard at a ball of it on the table.

She cannot hold her news for long.

'Did you know that Gabriel is leaving us at Christmas?' she bursts out.

'Is that so – after so many years?'

'Yes, Mrs. Maddocks, indeed; I could hardly believe my ears when he tell me. Ann bach, we shall look in the cups to see what will come for you.'

'Look in the teacups to see what will come to the harvest,' says Mary.

'Caton pawb! I know without the looking. First you will lose your barley, and afterwards Trefor will lose his oats. That's how it is, you see.'

When she has finished her tea Gwen swills her cup round three times and turns it upside-down in the saucer.

'To let the tears run down,' she says.

Mary is rather particular in her ways; she looks sideways at this. Gwen foretells a present and a gentleman visitor for herself.

'Now we'll try Ann's cup. Ah, she does not know how to shake up a good fortune in the tea-leaves!'

'It must be all nonsense if I make the fortune, good or bad, by shaking the cup.'

'Indeed,' says Gwen, looking very old-fashioned, 'and don't we all make our own fortunes? In your cup there are tears, tears, tears, and a land journey with a great surprise to you. Beware of danger by night; you are standing near a great misfortune, and soon you shall hear of a death.'

As she puts my cup down with a very solemn glance at me that makes us want to laugh, one of the hens outside gives a little crow like a young cockerel at dawn: Gwen begins to shake, and even Mary is a little pale.

'It is the truth that I have told you! Hark to the little bird, she knows best. When a hen crows in the yard, the time has come for one of the household to go through the dark.'

Mary laughs out loud.

'It is only an old saying, Miss Powys.'

'There is nothing so true as sayings, I tell you,' says

Gwen, who is very fanciful, like most of the Welsh folk.

'You are full of ideas,' I tells her.

'Yes, ideas. Listen, and I will tell you about the idea I saw in our yard last week. I was shutting up the hens; Trefor, he is in bed, Gabriel on the mountain with the sheep, and the girls, they are sleeping away. It was a very dark night, I was alone, and what did I see but a great dog glaring at me between me and the kitchen door! Ah, indeed, Mrs. Maddocks, my hair got up with fear, for it was bigger than any dog that walks the world we live in.

' "O Lord, save me from the devil," I cried, and on the sound of my voice the creature goes from my sight. I went in and shut all the doors and windows until the light of dawn. All night I did not close my eyes. Ah! indeed.'

'Perhaps it was a real dog,' says Mary, who is having hard work not to laugh.

'No, no, it was the devil,' answers Gwen.

'Well that may be, though myself I think the devil is too busy to have the doing of half that is laid to him. Folk speak badly of Llyn-tro; I have been there at night many a time and seen nothing.'

'Not for much would I go, even in full daylight. There my old father saw the spirit of the pool, and there the white otter swims.'

'And there my Georgie was nearly drowned.'

'And there are the biggest fish hereabouts,' I says.

And I thinks of the many times Gabriel and I have fished there together in the evenings when he was a boy just come to Tan y Bryn, and Wales was new to me.

I think the Welsh are fanciful folk that frighten none

but themselves by their tales, and though most of them are brave as lions, there are some, like Morgan, who will not stir a step after dark without company so be he can help it. One night I meet him coming home from Pentredwr when there is no moon: from the noise a person would think that three men are out walking, but there is only himself talking questions and answers very loud in three voices. He tells me three men pass safely where harm would fall to one. I ask him what harm could come to anybody in these quiet parts. He answers that if he knew he would not be affeared.

We have long seen the bread goes very fast from the larder. Such plain fare will not tempt Georgie and Jenny, and Charlie, with all his faults, is no thief of means or money; but Mary catches Morgan leaving the larder with something under his smock besides his dinner. She calls him back.

'What have you hidden away there?'

'Nought.'

'Let me see.'

It is half a loaf. She is vexed to find him stealing.

'I did not think it of you.'

Morgan mutters to himself, and at last he tells her that he is very affeared of dogs.

'They know when a man is like that,' he says in English, that he learned years gone by at service in Liverpool. 'When a dog see me she bark, bark like she was hungry, and would take a bite out of me. So every dog I meet her, I throw down a piece of bread.'

Mary is content to hear him speak her tongue, which he

will not often do, because, he says, it makes his blood rise to blow through his teeth in talking like we do. She cannot keep from laughing that a grown man who will tackle a bull with nought but a whip should go in fear of dogs. All she says is:

'Carry a stick, and don't you go stuffing all the hounds of the countryside with our baking.'

She keeps a good heart, but this is a sad harvest with the barley sprouting in the fields.

We go down to open the sheaves and spread them about in the air.

Gabriel and I pass in the market without a word or a sign.

We begin to load the barley.

The barn doors are opened wide only at harvest time, now they are propped with great stones that the carts may go in and out, and the barn seems very large inside without the half being full of hay. I work with Mary and Williams on the stack while Morgan, Charlie, and Lewis are loading in the fields. We have to keep Morgan and Lewis from each other, for whenever they get together they split words like two children. At night when we are at supper, we hear them at it hammer and tongs in the kitchen:

'What hast thou done today?' shouts one.

'Six times as much as thou!' answers the other, and the two of them would idle away the whole day without someone to eye them.

Charlie gives us all the fright of our lives: he is riding on the load when the wagon goes over a stone in the yard and with a yell he falls headfirst to the ground.

For a moment he does not move; we all rush to him, thinking to find him dead or dying, but his eyes are open and he smiles up at us. In a little while he gets upon his legs to go on with his work none the worse, as though his head were made of wood.

In the evening Mary has bread and cheese and beer laid out in the kitchen for the men – none eats so heartily as Charlie, and none looks so bright and humorous.

I have been to put my mother's grave straight after the high wind, and I walk back through the fields by moonlight. The wailing of the bull at Glanrafon comes to my ears while I am yet a field away; he smells a human being, though he is tied up in his pen, for the Pritchards are bound to be careful with a right of way running through their yard. When I come to the gate I open it and go in, not at all affeared, but I have hardly taken half a dozen steps when I see something like a great black shadow coming slowly to me. It is the bull, with his un-fastened chain dragging on his neck, turning his head from side to side and moaning as he walks. They are at the worst this time of the year, and with this in mind I lose no time in getting to the other side of the gate. He seems very quiet stood there, switching his tail, and staring at me through the bars with his eyes glinting in the moonlight, but I dare not pass through, for only last week Mr. Pritchard tells me he is very savage. I run round the front. There is a light upstairs and the Pritchards are going to bed. I fling a handful of dirt at the window, and Mrs. Pritchard puts her head out.

'Brenin Mawr! Is that Ann Goodman?'

'Yes, the bull is loose.'

She calls her husband and he comes down with a candle in his hand.

Not half an hour since, he says, the bull was safe in the pen, chained and made fast by himself.

'To be sure I had a peep at him. Ah, he is wicked! He looked at me. He never sleeps.'

He takes a pitchfork – I hear him chasing the bull into the pen, and the rattle of the chain.

When he comes back to me he is holding something in his hand: it is a shepherd's crook, and at Glanrafon there are no sheep.

I go home by the longer way – affeared.

Mary goes to her brother's for two days, taking the children with her.

I slide the bolts very early, going to bed with a stocking to knit for company. After the candle is out I hear a cart come into the yard, and there is a loud knocking on the kitchen door. I put on my shawl and call from the window to know who is there.

'Willy Preece from Cotterill's. Shall I put the horse up and come in? The rain is teeming down.'

I have time to dress and make up the fire, and wonder to myself what can have brought Willy over here, before he comes in, wet to the bone.

'I have a letter for you from the mistress.'

Gwladys Evans has written to ask me if I will go home at once to help my father, as there is scab in the sheep, and he cannot manage for himself.

Scab in my father's sheep!

Willy eats the bacon I give him and warms himself at the fire, filling the place with steam.

'What makes you so late?'

'I would have been here by midday, but beyond Trelech the horse shied and put me in the ditch; we broke an axle. But what time will you be ready in the morning?' he asks, as though there is nothing for me to do but to leave Twelve Poplars at a word from Gwladys Evans.

'I am not free to leave tomorrow. My father must wait until the next day.'

'Shepherd Goodman would wait till Domesday, but the mistress said to hurry.'

'No help for that – Mrs. Maddocks is from home, and you must stay here over tomorrow.'

Willy would argue, but I leave him a candle and go to bed. When Mary comes home, she is very angry, and the children cry.

'Why should you be for ever shifting yourself from pillar to post for the sake of a selfish old man that has no feeling for you at all? Stay here, Ann, and let his sheep go rotten with scab – his precious master can get help elsewhere.'

'I have thought there's something more behind Miss Evans's letter. How should my father's sheep come to have the scab?'

'That's true. Have you asked Willy Preece?'

'He will tell me nothing beyond what's in the letter.'

Mary makes a face.

'Well, Ann, if you feel you must go, you know you can come back when the wish takes you, and don't let yourself be put upon by John Goodman, father or no father. Not that you will, for you have his own temper hidden away. Maybe, too, it is better you should get away for a bit; there are some queer tales going about.'

Willy Preece is ready before it is properly light, though he takes so long over his breakfast that I might have had another half-hour in bed. But once we are on the road we hurry. At Trelech we change the horse for the master's mare, that trots faster between the shafts than any animal I know. We are half-way home before I ask Willy if the scab has spread badly.

'Three hundred odd,' he says, flicking the mare.

Three hundred! My breath is fairly taken away.

'How does it come to be so bad?' I ask, amazed. 'Three hundred means that it has spread for weeks without checking.'

Willy stares away over the mare's ears and says nothing, so that I could almost pinch him with vexation.

'Come, let me know what has happened. My father can tell the scab at a look; he would keep scabby sheep out of the flock.'

'Ay, he could tell right enough if he could see.'

'Willy Preece, do you mean my father is *blind*?'

'Often. Ann, Shepherd's taken to the bottle since your mother died.'

After a while he goes on:

'Scudamore had scabby sheep, and he was never over-careful. They strayed over into the master's meadows through a gap where there should have been a hurdle.'

'Is the master very vexed?'

87

'Ay, fair furious,' says Willy, 'but he hasn't said a word to Shepherd about going as far as I can make out.'

At Salus we stop to buy gunpowder for ointment. Willy has pressed the mare on the last few miles, so that she is black with sweat, and when I get home it is still light enough for me to see my garden overgrown with weeds. Our kitchen is like a pigsty.

My father is out with the sheep; after I have had something to eat I set to work to wash the pile of dirty dishes on the table. He comes in with a lantern about eleven.

'So you are back, after two days on the road. What were you doing at night?' he says.

'Oh! be silent,' I answer sharply, so vexed and tired that I hardly know where to turn.

My father mutters to himself:

'Here, take this lard and help me to make the ointment for the morning. Did you bring the powder?'

'Yes. Shall I use the lot?'

'Ay, there are two hundred sheep that need it.'

Willy made it out worse by a hundred, but this is bad enough.

I set the place to rights.

My father is trying tobacco water on the sheep: all day long there is a great cauldron over the fire, and our kitchen reeks of lard ointment and carbolic.

The scabby sheep are in Kirkham and Katy Hopkins, away from the whole; it is a sad thing to see them rubbing and picking at their wool with their necks and shoulders raw and red from the sores. Every day they are dressed by my father with Willy Preece and two young boys.

'Shall I come down to give you a hand?' I asks.

'Stay where you are,' my father answers angrily, 'and don't take so much on yourself.'

I do not go out much, but Mrs. Hill comes up to see me when she hears I am home. She is all in black that is not widow's mourning, and she seems pleased to take a cup of tea. We go in and sit by the fire.

'This is the first time I have been near the place since Myfanwy died.'

'A good thing, since my father kept it so dirty.'

'Is that so? And you was used to have it spotless.'

'There was enough cleaning out to do when I came back, and you must have seen the garden.'

'Yes,' says Mrs. Hill sadly, 'in the spring it was a picture.'

She looks down at her dress.

'Do you remember the May Dance, Ann? And now here we are sitting in black, the two of us. Have you heard about my poor little baby?'

'It is for her – the black?'

'Yes,' she says, beginning to cry, 'did no one tell you? And I thought my sorrow filled the world! She was taken poorly once or twice after you left home, and I see there was something wrong with her, for she was nothing more than a little bag of bones. Tom says, "Oh, it is nought but the rain, the sun, the heat, the cold; don't think so much about the child." He would not hear of the doctor. Ann, one night – the fifteenth of July it was – she had an awful fit and died before we could get a soul in to help. I put her in a warm bath and slapped her little hands and feet; it was no use, there was no life in her when Olwen brought the doctor.'

Mrs. Hill wrings her hands together till the knuckles show white as bone.

'There was an inquest after, and some very hard words were spoken. Tom has been a different man ever since. Sometimes, though we have been married but three years and I pity him with all my heart, it is all I can do to keep from hating him. Poor Tom! He meant no harm. Oh, it is a sad world, Ann!'

After a time I ask for news of Olwen.

'She left us; there was nothing for her to do. She went to Cotterill's to work for Miss Evans that always had a fancy for her. It is a good place, for she is a kind woman; Olwen always looks very content when she comes over to see us.'

So this was the master's news of Olwen!

Mrs. Hill will not stay long. She hurries off with her black frock fluttering round her, as thin as if she had half a mind to follow the baby.

All day long I am boiling, pounding, and mixing: my father uses gunpowder and lard for an ointment, tobacco water for a wash, and carbolic to stop the scab spreading. Every time he goes to Salus he brings more.

I help him to carry the bowls and buckets down to the pens; the men are waiting for us near the gates, and while they begin I go back again for the rest of the dressing. When I come back I start to work with them. One of them calls out to me:

'Don't you touch them, 'tisn't work for a woman – you might catch it yourself.'

'No more than us. Get on with what you are doing and leave the girl to work if she pleases,' says my father, without looking up.

We are at it until sundown, when we wash our hands and arms and go home. After supper there is more tobacco water to boil and more ointment to mix, and in my dreams I see a flock of scabby sheep driven into Llyn-tro by my father, who is waving a bottle.

Parson comes up in the rain with his umbrella, and his spaniel to keep him company. The wind is too strong for the umbrella; at the top of the hill, a step outside our gate, it is blown inside out. While he is pulling it right way about with one hand, and holding his hat on with the other, I bolt the door very quietly and hide at the back of the settle. After banging on the door three times loud enough to wake the dead, and peeping through every window, he goes away, leaving me in peace.

This afternoon it clears up a bit; Mrs. Somers and I go blackberrying together. She gives me news of her family. 'Owen is doing well in Monmouth, but Tom is a flighty boy; I always tell his father we shall come to see him deported. As for Chrissie, young as she is, she is a real bad girl!'

'She is very pretty and seems handy.'

'If she is pretty, what of that? So much the worse. It will be her undoing, I know, and as for handy, she is that; she has the makings of a thief.'

Mrs. Somers picks blackberries very quick and eats most of them.

When I find a good patch she leaves her own to strip mine bare. As fast as I move on she follows, talking all the time.

'What a deal of dying there has been this year! First

Sexton drowned in the river back in the winter, then your mother goes off in June, though I am sure you would have hindered her if you could, and then little Elsie Hill soon after. I should not wonder if Mrs. Hill herself went the next; she seems poorly. Half the parish looks ready for the grave with all the rain we've had.'

'It might be our turn next,' I says; Mrs. Somers goes on as if she has not heard me.

'And the different deaths people make! All my family go off very quiet, and I often wonder if I shall do the same. My father was a lovely man that died beautifully while carrying hay. He just dropped the fork and died. We were shorthanded that year too, and the morning before the funeral my sister and I were out in the meadow, doing his work.'

I go to another bush; Mrs. Somers follows.

'My sister died at forty-five. She was singing like an angel when she went, without any pain or struggle. Very quiet.'

And wherever I move she comes after me, telling me of the deaths in her family, till I know as much about them as if I had sat by all their bedsides and been to all their funerals. When it is time to go home she is surprised to find my basket quite full and her own more than half empty.

Olwen comes hurrying up the hill all out of breath, straight through the open door with her apron flying. She throws her arms round my neck tight enough to throttle me.

'Oh, Ann, my dear, I see Shepherd in the yard talking to the master, and I had the kitchen straight, so I ran up to you for a moment. I was affeared to come before lest he should be here,' she pants out.

Her hair, that she was used to keep in plaits down her back when I left Cotterill's, is twisted round her head and she wears a cap.

'Miss Evans makes me look like a grandmother!'

'No, Olwen, you look well and content.'

She is more lovely than anything that I have ever set my eyes on, but there is time enough for her to find that out.

'But, dear Ann, how sad you are!'

'It is nought but my mourning. Are you as happy as you were with Mrs. Hill?'

'Yes, indeed. The mistress is always kind; she never scolds but she is half laughing herself, though sometimes she talks until my head spins.'

'And the master?'

'I keep clear of him for fear of his terrible temper.'

'Is he unkind to you?'

She shakes her head.

'No, never, but he talks rough and looks miserable. He swears away to himself in Welsh all day long.'

'Maybe he isn't swearing if you cannot understand his tongue.'

'Oh yes, he is, between his teeth,' says Olwen laughing, 'and Miss Evans says, "Dal dy dafod".'

Willy Preece told me the meaning of that. I cannot help but smile.

'Then you don't like the master?'

'No, he is too rough. Nobody likes him in these parts.'

'It does seem nobody has a good word for him.'

'He is terrible hard on his men, Ann, and on his animals too, if it suits him. Last week he flogged one of the horses up the hill with a load of roots that Willy said was more than enough for two. The mistress put her fist through the wire net over the larder window, she was that upset. "For shame, brother!" she screamed out in English so that all the world could hear.'

'What did he say?'

'He shouted something and threw the whip into the pigsties. I couldn't understand because they always speak Welsh to each other.

'Oh, Ann, the mistress is a good woman; she sings hymns beautiful and plays the harmonium in the parlour on Sunday afternoons.'

'And does the master sing hymns too?'

Olwen laughs out loud.

'No, he goes to sleep! Ann, they say Welsh folk are near, yet your mother was Welsh and she was kind to me, while Shepherd will never give me a word. Miss Evans is good to everybody, even tramps and beggars. Many of that sort come round for meals regular as washing days: they are given everything we have ourselves; they sit on the cobbles outside the back door, and when they have finished they hand me the dish and go off without a word.'

'And what does the master say to that?'

'The mistress always tells me to look out for him; if I see him coming they make off to hide, for he makes trouble when he catches them. He come in sudden through the dairy door once when there was a tramp that Miss Evans was giving bread and butter; we pushed the tramp into the larder while the master passed, and when we went to let him out we found he had gone with sausages and two

pounds of butter that was put by for young Mrs. Williams because her husband had been poorly.'

'I should think Miss Evans gave over a bit after that.'

'No, she said there are good and bad tramps, same as other folk.'

She gets up to go, but I catch at her.

'Wait, Olwen – tell me, you must have heard – is it true that my father drinks overmuch these days?'

'Folk say he does.'

'Can't you tell me any more than that?'

'Yes, only don't look at me so sharp, dear Ann, and I'll tell you all I know. The day after Shepherd found scab in the sheep I was washing potatoes in the brook, and I heard Mrs. Hill talking to the mistress.

' "Why doesn't your brother get rid of him?" she asks. "He was never an overpatient master, by all accounts. Only last week Tom found Shepherd in the hedge, sleeping it off." '

'Go on, Olwen bach, what more?'

'I splashed my hands in the water so they should know someone was there, but they went on talking. The mistress answered:

' "My brother wouldn't hear of it, no more would I. The man was here for years before us."

' "Yes," says Mrs. Hill, in a kinder voice, "he has passed most of his life in that cottage, and he was born in the workhouse at Salus."

'I could not help but hear, Ann!'

'What of that?' I says.

Olwen puts her hand on mine.

'Miss Evans goes on: "He brought his wife there, out of

Wales. Oh, we Welsh aren't as black as you paint us, Mrs. Hill. My brother is a hard man in many ways, but he would never get rid of John Goodman."'

I do not know what comes over me that I cry out:

'Ni fedrwch gael ei debyg yn Lloegr!'

Olwen stares at me.

'Why, what does that mean?'

'I hardly know myself.'

At dusk I pass the master in the fields.

'Nos da, Ann Goodman.'

'Nos da, Evan ap Evans.'

I sit waiting for my father to come in until midnight, then I take the lantern and go to look for him. There is no moon. Beyond my lantern-light it is pitch dark, and as I reach the bottom it begins to rain. My father is lying on the far side of the stream as still as if he were dead; neither shakes nor shouts rouse him up. I leave him, and run back to Cotterill's for Willy Preece. He is coming down the granary steps very softly, with his fishing rod in his hand, and he calls out my name, affeared at seeing me out at this hour when only poachers are abroad.

'Hush!' I whispers, with my eyes on a lighted window. 'Come and help me to carry my father up the hill.'

As we creep out of the yard the master's dog gives a yowl that brings him to the window, candle in hand.

'Who's there?' he calls.

'Run! He'll be down in another minute!' says Willy.

My father has not moved; together we get him home, though the hill has never seemed so long. We look down on him, full length on the settle, and Willy tells me he will never be fit for work in the morning.

'I'll be there to do his share.'

'But, Ann, it's not a woman's work.'

'I have done it before now.'

Willy says no more, he has other things afoot. He goes away quietly, but not to his bed.

In the morning my father is still sleeping as I go out, turning the key on him. All the men stare when they see me coming with the buckets and no shepherd. They ask where he is.

'At home, as you know very well. There's not an hour's work in him, so I'll do it for him. Now let us settle to.'

None gainsays me.

Ill luck will have it that the master comes to look at the sheep.

'No shepherd this morning, Preece?' he asks, lifting his brows. Then he catches sight of me, and coming over stands before me.

'Ann!'

'Good day, Master.'

'Give over this minute.'

'That I will not.'

'Thou must,' says he, 'I'm going to do the work myself. But thou shalt hand me the stuff.'

'Master, let me do it. It is my father's work, and he is asleep in the kitchen at home. Let me.'

'What is that to me?' he cries. 'Stand out of the way, Ann bach, and thou shalt see what a fine shepherd was lost to make an ordinary farmer.'

He strips off his coat and rolls up his sleeves: to see him set about it I remember my mother was used to say that as a young boy he was a shepherd on the mountains.

'Art happy to be home?' he asks.

'Yes.'

'Wert content to see me this morning?'

'I never was more vexed,' I says, half laughing.

'From my heart I thank thee,' he says under his breath.

When I get home I find my father mixing ointment. 'You can be useful, it seems,' he grunts. 'You had best come down with me every day. If they do well, they will be over it in a fortnight.'

'One thing, I know, they will never do well without a shepherd. The way those boys handle them is pitiful to see.'

'What! After all I have taught them! I'll show them round,' my father cries angrily.

Today I let my father know I am not going back to Twelve Poplars before the spring.

'Do as you please,' he answers.

It is hard that whatever I do should be of so little account.

The master is ploughing. The crows follow the furrow, flying round him, and settling on the red earth where he has passed.

His eyes are on his work; only at the turn he sees me stood watching him in the shadow of the hedge, and as he moves down the field his words come back to me, though they are softly spoken in the tongue he was born to:

'What art thou doing there all alone?'

It is the truth that I answer:

'Waiting for thee.'

It is dark when he leaves the plough and, coming to me, looks down in my face:

'Fy nghariad, the waiting is over,' he says, and with his two hands draws me to him.

We shall be married before the trees are bare, for there is no need of waiting.

In a letter Mary tells me Gabriel left Tan y Bryn last week without warning.

Autumn has come: her sheep are from the mountains, and Morgan is threshing the barley in the long dark evenings.

It seems like some peace at last!

(END OF ANN'S BOOK)

Evan ap Evans was never married to his shepherd's daughter; before the trees were bare, she was lying in Salus churchyard, and his name and Gabriel Ford's were on the lips of all the countryside.

There is a stone on the river bank with a rail around it to keep off the cattle. It was placed there by the master opposite the deep pool where Ann was found, her body wrapped in water weeds, her head no more than an inch or two from the surface.

On her temple was a great wound that cried aloud for justice. The cry was taken up all along the Border, and rang in the ears of Evan ap Evans, who loved her, as he avowed, above all things on earth.

Suspicion was divided between him and Gabriel Ford, but while the Welshman was at hand to bear the load of it

with all eyes fixed upon the hideous burden, the Englishman, from the time he left Tan y Bryn, was never again seen by the living. None knew of his goings and comings, and only the testimony of Mary Maddocks saved Evan ap Evans from arrest. But while he was not held guilty in the eyes of the law, neither lack of evidence nor lack of motive could shield him from the rage of the country-folk; his violence and the distrust which his ways had fostered, gave rise to wild brutal rumours which even today are looked upon as truth.

Though Gabriel was undoubtedly the murderer and Evan ap Evans the lover, his unpopularity reached a climax which, together with a grief so sharp that he could no longer endure the neighbourhood, caused him to part with Cotterill's.

He died, it is said, in Canada.

These are the facts which can be gathered from the tangle of traditions and tales in a district where suspicions are truths and rumours evidence, facts which are borne out in the little ruled book where Gabriel is branded and where a darker pen runs beside Ann's quill, tracing a noose which, had it lain to hand, would have hanged him as surely as he deserved such a death, and which is like a long-hidden key to a door that has rotted away.

In this book some may see only the evidence of a guilt which never came to light until its power was as dead as the hand that wrote it, or at the most, the insignificant prelude to a commonplace disaster. Also there may be those who will discern the subtler underlying narrative that bound the days together, the record of a mind rather than of actions, a mind which though clear in itself was never conscious of the

two nations at war within it. Here is represented the entire history of the Border, just as the living Ann must have represented it herself – that history which belongs to all border lands and tells of incessant warfare.

Wales against England – and the victory goes to Wales; like Evan ap Evans, the awakened Celt cries: 'Cymru am byth!' with every word she writes.

Those that can follow this will see that the story begins and ends with the book; for them there will be no need to follow the bodily fate of the men and women who people it. Complete and triumphant, it stands untouched by word of mouth fed from the rusty memories of folk long since dead who would have decked it out according to their own opinions and allotted tails and haloes as their lively fancy pleased.

All old stories, even the authenticated, even the best remembered, are painted in greys and lavenders – dim, faint hues of the past which do no more than whisper of the glory of colour they once possessed. Yet live awhile in these remote places where these pale pictures were painted, and something of their first freshness will return to them, if only in the passing of a homestead or the mowing of a field. You will come to know how the dead may hold tenure of lands that were once theirs, and how echoes of their lives that are lost at a distance linger about their doorways. Here among the hills and valleys, the tall trees and swift rivers, the bland pastures and sullen woods, lie long shadows of things that have been.

But new furrows are ploughed in old fields, harvests are sown and gathered, and names that sprang from the red earth itself have died away to a faint murmur which only native ears attuned may hear.

It is well that men's doings, like the leaves after their season, fall to the earth, and beneath the boughs, crowded with fresh green growth, lie buried and forgotten.

Foreword by Catrin Collier

Born in Pontypridd, Catrin Collier now lives in Swansea.
She is the author of twenty-seven novels, including the
Swansea Girls trilogy, the Pontypridd set historical saga,
which began with *Hearts of Gold*, and which was adapted
as a BBC series, and *Beggars and Choosers* (2003), set
against the backdrop of the Tonypandy Riots. *Tiger Bay
Blues* is published in 2006.

Cover image by Peggy Whistler

LIBRARY OF WALES

The Library of Wales is a Welsh Assembly Government project designed to ensure that all of the rich and extensive literature of Wales which has been written in English will now be made available to readers in and beyond Wales. Sustaining this wider literary heritage is understood by the Welsh Assembly Government to be a key component in creating and disseminating an ongoing sense of modern Welsh culture and history for the future Wales which is now emerging from contemporary society. Through these texts, until now unavailable or out-of-print or merely forgotten, the Library of Wales will bring back into play the voices and actions of the human experience that has made us, in all our complexity, a Welsh people.

The Library of Wales will include prose as well as poetry, essays as well as fiction, anthologies as well as memoirs, drama as well as journalism. It will complement the names and texts that are already in the public domain and seek to include the best of Welsh writing in English, as well as to showcase what has been unjustly neglected. No boundaries will limit the ambition of the Library of Wales to open up the borders that have denied some of our best writers a presence in a future Wales. The Library of Wales has been created with that Wales in mind: a young country not afraid to remember what it might yet become.

Dai Smith